CW00968085

Praise for Mackenzie McKade's
Take Me Again

"Mackenzie McKade is a truly gifted author. Her stories never disappoint. Take Me Again was a passionate story that will captivate any reader. I can not wait to read whatever Ms. McKade has in store for us next. It should be just as intoxicating as this fabulous romantic adventure."

~ *Kimberley Spinney, Ecataromance*

"...This book should come with a warning label: sexy cowboy and his bad boy ways will hold you hostage to his sizzling delights as he tames the woman of his dreams! I look forward to another book in this delightful series."

~ *Shannon, The Romance Studio*

"Mackenzie McKade brings these characters and their troubles to life in this emotionally captivating read. TAKE ME AGAIN delves into the trouble Tracy would face trying to establish herself as a competent vet and still allows readers to get to know her as a woman with all the hopes, dreams and fears that go along with her responsibilities. ...I really enjoy how Ms. McKade brings Cord and Caitlyn into this story and infuses so much humor through Caitlyn's quick witted fun loving personality and how she keeps the men on their toes."

~ *Chrissy Dionne, Romance Junkies*

Look for these titles by
Mackenzie McKade

Now Available:

Take Me Again

Mackenzie McKade

A SAMHAIN PUBLISHING, LTD. publication.

Samhain Publishing, Ltd.
577 Mulberry Street, Suite 1520
Macon, GA 31201
www.samhainpublishing.com

Take Me Again
Copyright © 2009 by Mackenzie McKade
Print ISBN: 978-1-60504-428-6
Digital ISBN: 978-1-60504-360-9

Editing by Angela James
Cover by Natalie Winters

This book is a work of fiction. The names, characters, places, and incidents are products of the writer's imagination or have been used fictitiously and are not to be construed as real. Any resemblance to persons, living or dead, actual events, locale or organizations is entirely coincidental.

All Rights Are Reserved. No part of this book may be used or reproduced in any manner whatsoever without written permission, except in the case of brief quotations embodied in critical articles and reviews.

First Samhain Publishing, Ltd. electronic publication: January 2009
First Samhain Publishing, Ltd. print publication: November 2009

Dedication

To my wonderful critique partners Sharis Mayers and Jennifer Ray. Thank you! Your support and friendship means the world to me.

Chapter One

Tension crawled across Dolan Crane's shoulders. Not only were his tendons tight, they burned like a sonofabitch. Even his fingers felt stiff as he reached for the key and switched off the truck's engine. For a moment he didn't move. Instead he dragged in a weighted breath.

"What a fucked-up day," he grumbled on an exhale. A set of headlights flashed through the windshield, blinding him. He squinted against their brilliance and the starry night.

The thought of restarting his vehicle and heading home surfaced but didn't linger. Maybe a night out on the town was what he needed to unwind. He rolled his shoulders listening to the crackle and pop as he leaned his head from side to side. With a little luck, he'd find a sweet thing to cuddle up to and ease his body and mind.

Of course that might be impossible because he was on call this weekend. Doc Zimmerman was off again for a weekend of R and R. The seasoned veterinarian was nearing retirement and Dolan was setting himself up to swoop in and take over. Yet the events of today could throw a wrench into his plans. He watched a shooting star blaze across the sky, burning out in a blink of an eye. For a second he wondered if there was anything significant between the star and his career.

Pulling a weary breath, he held it before releasing it in one gush. "Dammit." He slammed a palm on the steering wheel.

This afternoon he'd lost a million-dollar colt. By the time Victor Tate had called him it had been too late to save the animal. However, his client didn't see it quite that way.

The man was furious.

It wasn't that Dolan took Tate's ranting to heart; the proof was in the evidence. Lady Liberty had dropped the foal before his arrival, which had been only ten minutes after he'd received the call. Yet the sonofabitch thought money could buy anything, even life. The umbilical cord had been wrapped around the colt's neck. He had saved the mare from bleeding to death, but even that hadn't been enough. Not to Tate or Dolan.

Down on his knees, he had tried to breathe life back into the foal, knowing it was futile. A sense of helplessness had nearly overwhelmed him. He hated that feeling almost as much as he regretted losing the colt.

"Not your fault." He tried once again to convince himself that there had been nothing he could have done.

Would others see it that way? He sure as hell hoped so.

Trying to establish a career in Santa Ysabel, California, the home of some of the finest racehorses, he didn't need setbacks like this. Losing a potential racer was like slitting one's throat. His hand went to his neck as if guarding it from the invisible knife he felt pressed against his skin.

"Let it go." He lowered his hand and blinked hard trying to clear his mind and focus on the muffled cry of a steel guitar coming from the home before him. He finger combed his ebony hair and grabbed his hat off the passenger seat.

Loud music flooded the cab as he opened the truck door and stepped out. A warm summer breeze whipped around him, carrying with it the sweet scent of magnolias. Low vibrating bass echoed in his head as he secured his vehicle before slipping his keys deep into the pocket of his jeans. With both hands he squared his Stetson on his head and tugged the rim forward before heading for the front door.

Jester Norton was known for his house parties. Everyone was invited for a weekend of poker, billiards, dancing, plenty of liquor and several unoccupied bedrooms for those seeking a little extracurricular activity. The last thought put a bounce in Dolan's step. He needed to get laid. Wrap his arms around something other than his problems.

As was customary on a Friday night, the place was packed. The noise level bordered on offensive; then again it could be his rotten mood. He tried to brush away his edginess, but it stuck to him like glue. Maybe he should just go home. Even as the thought entered his mind he continued to stroll into the great room. A kitchen, living and dining room all meshed into one big adult playroom.

His home away from home.

What could he say? He liked the ladies. Always had—always would.

Yet most daddies around here guarded their daughters from him. His reputation preceded him. Bachelor. Carouser. The fact he dabbled a little in ménage a trois probably didn't help his cause with the fathers, but the ladies seemed to find his soiled reputation exciting. He pushed through the crowd, his boots clicking against the polished wood floor as he scoped out the pickings for tonight.

Several couples were on the makeshift dance floor swaying to the gentle beat of a ballad that just started, while a group of cowboys surrounded a table laden with snacks from chips and salsa to hot wings and other appetizers. Even more people were lingering around the bar and overflowing into other areas of the house, including the basement where the real fun usually began.

Amy Waters, a short little blonde he had shared a night or two with, gave him a come-hither smile. Tight jeans and a halter top said she was ready for a night of fun.

Stroking the tip of his mustache, he murmured, "First things first."

Without delay he made a beeline straight for the bar, eyes narrowing on his immediate goal—a drink. Not a smart thing to do since he was on call. Yet one drink wouldn't hurt him.

He leaned in, placing his forearms on the marble surface. "Hit me with a double, Jester."

Okay. Make it two drinks. With a little luck there wouldn't be an emergency tonight.

The barrel-chested man reached for a half-full bottle of whiskey, his other hand going towards a glass. He tipped the bottle, golden liquor splashing over the ice. A look of concern tugged at his friend's brows. "Bad day?"

Dolan breathed in the heady scent of whiskey with a thirst that surprised him. No sipping and savoring the taste tonight. He curled his fingers around the drink and brought it to his lips. "Seen better," he mumbled against the cool crystal.

Mouth watering, he was about to down the drink when he heard, "Move over, cowboy," from someone down the bar.

Deep and rich, almost hypnotic, the woman's delivery was like silk gliding over his skin. Images of hot naked bodies pressed together flashed into his head. His cock jerked against his zipper. The result was a flood of tingles surging throughout his body.

Well, that had never happened before. With three little words a stranger had extinguished his foul mood and fired up his libido.

Soft laughter caressed his ears. The denim across his hips tightened even more. Someone must have turned the heater on, making the summer night even warmer. He tugged at the collar of his T-shirt. Lowering his glass, he glanced down the bar for the one who had evoked such a heady reaction within him.

A statuesque redhead stepped up to the bar four people down from him. He couldn't see her face clearly, but the brief view of her profile, porcelain skin, a slightly tipped nose, and a stubborn jaw, made him want to see more. Long, wavy hair the color of copper flowing down her back only added to his need. His palms itched with the yearning to feel the silky threads glide through his fingers.

Jester gawked alongside the rest of the horny men staring in her direction. "Fuckin' hot," he murmured more to himself than anyone in particular.

Dolan had to agree. The woman was built like a Rolls Royce. Expensive curves and dips exactly where they should be, but there was a casual air about her. She looked comfortable and confident in a short leather skirt and spaghetti strap tank top.

"Who is she?" he asked.

Nonchalantly, he leaned back to get a better look. Damned if the guy next to him had the same idea, blocking his view. Taking a step backward he glimpsed something black and lacy before the guy next to him once again shifted in his line of sight.

Was that a garter? A smile tugged at Dolan's mouth. He loved garters, especially taking them off.

Jester's grin widened, too. "Never seen her before. Guess I'd better exercise my rights as the host and welcome her to the neighborhood." Wagging his brows, he wasted no time making tracks down the bar. "Hey darlin'. What's your poison?"

13

"Bourbon on the rocks," she answered, wetting her lips. Dolan's cock jerked again.

Now that was interesting. No beer or fruity drink for her. He almost chuckled, recalling what one of his old college buddies had once told him. "Women who drink whiskey are unique. You have to talk dirty to them while challenging them intellectually."

That certainly could be arranged.

Of course, every man in the place was probably planning to take her home. The glass he held clicked as he set the full drink down. This was one woman he had to meet. He stepped away from the bar without a second thought.

As he drew near a hint of powder rose above the scents of alcohol and aftershave. With her back now to him, he took the time to scrutinize her long legs, firm thighs and an ass that made him pause.

Oh yeah. That's what he was talking about. He could visualize his hands resting on those cheeks, parting them. A shudder raked up his spine with the sinful thought of invading that tight rosebud. An unexpected surge of blood rushed his groin. He sucked in a quick breath through clenched teeth, trying to dash his wayward thoughts. Last thing he needed was to have a hard-on when he introduced himself.

Before he could close the distance between them and make his move, the lanky cowboy to her right asked, "Dance with me?"

The shorter man to her left said, "She's dancing with me."

The air thickened around them. Add to that their rigid stance and it was clear they were prepared to fight for the chance to hold her in their arms. Their glares locked and in unison both reached for her.

Dolan heard no fear in her voice when she said, "Uh—boys? No reason to ruin the night." In fact, amusement laced her

14

laughter as she pressed a palm to each of their chests and with amazing strength wedged them from her. That's when he noticed the definition in her arms. Damned if he didn't find that sexy too. His feet continued to carry him forward.

"How 'bout I dance with both of you. You first," she said to the taller of the men. Spinning on the toes of her boots, she came face to face with Dolan.

He looked into turquoise eyes dancing with humor that immediately turned sultry as her eyelashes fell half-mast. Never breaking their connection, he touched the brim of his Stetson. Her full lips parted as if she intended to speak, but before she could make a sound, the cowboy next to her scooped her hand into his and pulled her onto the dance floor.

Strangely, a sense of loss swept over Dolan. For a moment, he was speechless and it appeared his feet didn't work any better. Like an idiot he just stood there. Add the fact that he couldn't keep his eyes off her and he felt more the fool.

That's when it happened. She glanced over her shoulder and smiled. Every muscle inside him melted. It took only a moment for him to realize he was staring at her like some lovesick high school boy.

Whoa there, partner.

He mentally pulled himself together. Tired, he rationalized and slowly headed back to the bar to retrieve his drink. Glass cool against his palm, he raised the amber to his lips and took a sip. The whiskey burned so good down his throat. With a clink he placed the glass back on the bar and scanned the crowd. Damned if his gaze wasn't pulled back to the dance floor.

Wow. That little filly could move.

Her body swayed, her feet not missing a step as the cowboy guided her around the floor. As she twirled, her hair floated on the breeze. He couldn't help wondering what it would smell like

15

if he buried his nose deep into its softness.

What was wrong with him? He rubbed a palm over his eyes. Maybe he just needed to leave and go to bed. Before he removed his hand, the image of sexy turquoise eyes popped into his mind. Once again his gaze was drawn to the dance floor by some invisible force. He found himself taking a step toward her.

On the tail end of a spin, she glanced his way. Their eyes met and for a second it felt like time stood still. It was just him—her. Something strange and provocative passed between them.

What the hell?

He was left hanging onto the moment as the cowboy who held her whisked her away and broke their contact. Dolan took another step toward the dance floor. Something was not right. His heart was racing. His breath hitched as he attempted to reel in his emotions.

His full attention was on one redhead who danced seductively to the rhythm of the music. What he would give to have those hips moving against his, her arms bound around him—

A slap on the back ripped him out of the bewitchment she had cast upon him. He blinked, sounds and sights coming back into focus, as well as Rowdy Jackson, a friend from Colorado, standing beside him.

He frowned. "You okay?"

"Hell yes." Dolan's voice rose with recognition. He jutted his hand out in welcome. "Thought you were coming in tomorrow."

Rowdy was relocating from Denver. No one would know that the six-foot cowboy was a genius with a computer. He had exchanged riding broncos for a keyboard. A local company was paying him a bundle to overhaul their current system.

"Wrapped things up early. Nothing in the Rocky Mountains keeping me, so I hit the road." Rowdy scanned his surroundings. "Stopped by the house, but you weren't there. We still good for this weekend?" He was bunking with Dolan until the closing of his home scheduled for Monday morning.

Rowdy's grin deepened when his gaze lit on the dance floor. "Well I'll be damned." Stripping his Stetson off his head, he started to speak but the ringing of a cell phone interrupted him. On the second ring, his friend glanced down at the phone hanging from Dolan's waist. "Going to answer that?"

Well fuck. So much for a night out on the town. Dolan wedged the cell from his belt, flipped the cover open, and pressed it to his ear.

"*Crane?*" There was urgency in the caller's breathless voice.

Dolan gripped the telephone. "Yes."

"G-grain. Mare got into—" In the background he heard the young male cry out in distress as he dropped the telephone and then scrambled for it.

"Hello?" Dolan stole a glance at the woman of his dreams. Heavy eyelids were shuttered as she stared up at her partner as he spoke to her. "Who is this?"

"Wood. Travis Wood." The seventeen-year-old sounded scared and close to tears, judging by his quivering voice.

It was just a guess, but Dolan figured one of their mares had gotten into the grain. Not a good thing for a horse. "How bad is it?" Dammit. He could see his opportunity to spend the evening with the redhead slip through his fingers.

"Don't know. God. I-I can't believe this. I just turned my back for a moment. Dad is going to kill me. Can you come quick?"

"Be there in fifteen." Dolan turned to Rowdy. "Gotta go.

17

Sorry." Stuffing his hand into his jeans, he pulled out a house key and tossed it to his friend. "Make yourself at home." Without another word, he turned and rushed for the exit.

As the music ended, Tracy Marx stepped out of the cowboy's arms. Damn. What was his name? Was it John? Paul? George? Ringo? A silent chuckle tickled her throat.

With a sultry expression, he smiled down at her, sliding his palms up her bare arms. "How about another dance?"

"Dance?" She glanced at him not really seeing him. Shamefully, her mind wandered to another—one who'd left her wanting with a single look. The flame had sparked again when their eyes had met once more.

The whole time they'd sashayed across the floor all she could think of was the dark-haired cowboy who appeared out of nowhere. Even when Tom—*yes, Tom was his name*—had suggested they find a quieter place to talk all she could think of was blue-black hair and eyes dark as the night.

She scanned the room in search of her mystery man. Disappointment hit her hard when the spot where he had last stood was vacant. Reluctantly, she drew her attention back to Tom and his question. "Can't. Promised the next dance to—"

Crap. Forgot that guy's name too. She never had problems with her memory. Guess she had too much on her mind tonight.

The stout cowboy she had met earlier sidled up to her. "Charles," he said slipping an arm around her waist to pull her back firmly against his body. "My turn."

Tom stiffened. His brows tugged down into a scowl. For a moment, she thought he might raise a ruckus.

Men were gutsier then she remembered. They could be so primitive. Give them a drink or two and they became throwbacks from the Stone Age, fighting to resolve all their disagreements.

Tracy released a pent-up breath when Tom finally tipped his hat. "Later, sweetheart."

"Not if I have anything to say about it," Charles whispered in her ear.

Her equilibrium was shot to hell when he twirled her around and into his embrace. His feet immediately started to move to the quick beat of the music. Lightheaded, she missed the first step, but caught the next one to glide across the floor. He held her confidently, guiding her into each move easily.

"So, little lady, where you from?"

Little? She was five-eight, one or two inches shorter than him. Judging by his solid build the man was a bull-rider. Of course, she'd been wrong before. "Nebraska," she answered.

Tracy wasn't prepared when Charles abruptly spun her twice, drawing her firmly against him on the final spin. But it was the knee wedged between her legs that made her attention perk up. He rubbed his thigh up hers. The large bulge in his jeans pressed against her abdomen was difficult to miss. The man was aroused. He ground his hips to hers emphasizing the point before giving her a devilish grin.

Good ol' Charlie expected a reaction, but she wasn't biting. *Not my type.* Besides she was just here to burn off some energy. Tomorrow was a big day for her.

Yeah. He might give her a good ride, but she was looking for something more, someone who could ignite a fire inside her with just a look. Someone like the cowboy she'd exchanged glances with before hitting the dance floor. Her thoughts wandered back to a pair of dark eyes. The bad boy persona the dark-haired cowboy wore screamed excitement and adventure. That's what she wanted—hungered for.

A light kiss pressed to her neck brought her back to the

man who held her. "I've never seen you here before. Visiting?" His voice deepened as he rubbed his cheek against hers. The scent of sandalwood was strong. She preferred the light spicy scent of the dark-haired cowboy. It left her speechless and horny.

What was she saying? She didn't even know the guy.

"Yes. No." Truthfully, she wasn't sure. Her uncle had promised to help her establish a business in Santa Ysabel. Back in Omaha her mother had agreed to watch Sheldon until she found a home and babysitter. Again her chest squeezed.

It had been nine months since her sister's unexpected death. Shelly had been thrown from a horse. Her head had struck the only rock in the field. Tracy's ex hadn't appreciated becoming a parent so soon, but she had no alternative. Her mother had enough health problems of her own. Lois Marx had a bad heart. Besides Tracy was Sheldon's godmother and she loved the three-year-old as if he were her own. Leaving Nebraska was a new start for both of them.

Charles chuckled. "Which is it?"

"What?" Blinking hard, she tried to recall what he asked. She had shit for a memory tonight. What she needed to do was pull herself together, but it was difficult when she had so much on her mind. Other than college, she'd never been this far away from home, never been alone. Even married she had lived only a mile away from home.

He eased his hold putting enough distance between them so he stared into her eyes. "Are you visiting or staying?"

Multiple choices—this should be easy. Yet she remained silent pondering his question.

Just pick one, a voice in her head chastised.

"Staying," she heard herself say.

There, that wasn't so hard.

Yet saying it aloud authenticated her decision and she wasn't sure it was the right one. What if she couldn't find enough work? What if the people in California didn't like her? She was a country-girl born and raised. What did she know about dealing with people of influence? What she did know were animals, especially horses.

An ear-to-ear grin tugged at Charles's mouth. His hand fell to rest on her ass. "Need a place to stay?"

His innuendo didn't escape her. She cocked a brow, grasping his hand to guide it back to her waist. "Got it covered, but thanks for the invitation."

His palm worked its way back down to ride the top of her ass. "Does that mean tonight is out?"

Men! She shook her head in disbelief.

Relief surfaced when the song came to an end. Hastily, she stepped out of his embrace. "Thanks, but I have plans tonight. Now if you'll excuse me." Cutting through the crowd, she avoided Tom when he nodded at her, choosing instead to head for the line growing outside the bathroom door. It was as good as any place for her to catch her bearings.

Tracy probably shouldn't have ventured outside her uncle's estate tonight. But her fifteen-year-old cousin had recommended she check out Jester's party. She didn't want to speculate how Laurie knew about this place. From everything Tracy'd seen so far it was a meat market and the perfect place to pick up a one-night stand, which was exactly what she was in the mood for, but it would have to wait.

There would be questions if she didn't come home tonight. An inquisition was something she didn't need to deal with. But she might have stood a cross-examination for the tall, dark cowboy. She took one more look around the room and wondered if her mystery man had gone down the flight of stairs to the basement.

"Looking for someone, sugar?" The whiskey-smooth male's voice sounded familiar.

She turned and a smile fell across her face. "Rowdy."

He wrapped his arms around her waist and raised her off her feet to twirl her around, nearly knocking over two other women in line. They cast a disgruntled look, but remained quiet as she slithered down his firm body, raising her skirt to where it barely covered her butt. She gave the hem a tug as he settled her on her feet.

He held her at arm's length. "I couldn't believe it was you waltzing around the dance floor. What the hell brings you to this neck of the woods?"

"I could say the same to you." She took in his athletic build, knowing exactly what hid beneath his cotton shirt; lean strong muscles. Long powerful legs were encased in snug denim that rode low on his lean hips. Yep. She remembered the bulge between his thighs too. Hastily she jerked her gaze back to his face.

A wicked grin fell across his face. He pulled her back into his arms, giving her a squeeze. "Here with someone?" he murmured against her ear.

"No."

"That makes two of us." He nibbled on her earlobe. "How about I take you home, tie you up and have my way with you?"

Chills raced across her skin as his hair tickled her neck. The man was gorgeous. Peeking from beneath his Stetson, sandy blond hair framed his tanned face.

"Yes" was on the tip of her tongue. His sexy invitation almost made her forget she needed to call it a night soon.

"Sounds delicious, but I'll have to pass. I work tomorrow."

His lips were soft trailing along her jaw line and cheeks, until his mouth whispered across hers. "Are you sure?" He caressed his tongue along the crease of her lips. "If I recall, we made some sweet music together."

Sweet music? That was an understatement.

Rowdy had been her first lover after the divorce. She had been scared and uncertain. He had been patient and understanding and joked around to make her feel comfortable. They had talked, but more importantly he had listened, asking questions and appearing genuinely interested in her plans for the future.

Little touches here—kisses there—and before the night ended she found herself locked in his arms, revealing some of her deepest desires. At the moment there hadn't seemed to be any danger in her frankness about her sexual desires. He was a stranger passing through town. Hell. After a couple of drinks and another tumble between the sheets, she had even told him about her darkest fantasy—a ménage a trois.

To her surprise he hadn't been judgmental. He didn't make her feel as if her wayward thoughts were disturbing or wrong. In fact, he appeared to be aroused by her confession, taking her in his arms and making passionate love to her once more.

Embarrassment heated her face. *I can't believe I revealed that fantasy.*

He smoothed a hand gently over her cheek as if he could sense her sudden discomfort. "It's me, baby." He looked at her with warm brown eyes. "I can make your fantasies come true." He pressed his mouth to her ear. "All of them," he whispered.

Oh God. He remembered.

A spark sputtered low in her belly. The burn matched the heat flaring across her cheeks. Surely he was just teasing her.

23

Even still, the thought of two men worshipping her body all night long was beyond exciting. It was downright sinful.

"Can't." She swallowed hard. "Not tonight."

Damn. Damn. Damn. It was already getting late and she didn't want to disturb her uncle's household. She didn't miss the disappointment on his face as he released her.

"When?"

"Maybe Monday. My weekend is booked solid."

"Monday it is. Give me your number." He pulled his cell phone out of his pocket and punched in her number as she rattled it off. "I'll call you with the directions to my house." He caressed her cheek. "Are you up for anything?" There was a spark of devilment in his eyes.

Anything?

"Yes," slipped from her mouth before she could think twice.

"I promise it will be a night dedicated solely to your pleasure." He kissed her softly. "Until Monday."

Eyes closed, lips still puckered, she murmured, "Uh-huh." He tapped her on the nose. Her eyelids rose.

He winked. "Later, baby."

She sighed low and long as she watched him walk away. Later couldn't come anytime too soon.

Chapter Two

A hint of last night's tension hid beneath a cloak of fatigue. Eyes closed, Dolan stretched across his bed, arms extending above his head. A dull twinge slid along his shoulders. Groaning, he grabbed a pillow and placed it over his face to shut out the morning light creeping in through parted curtains. The crisp scent of newly washed sheets filled his nostrils.

What he'd give to lie there and do nothing, but the day was calling to him. He had a full schedule. Not only did he have several appointments scheduled, he had to inoculate Misty Dawn and Taylor Tweeds. Two of several race horses his cousin had inherited through his recent marriage and Cord had mentioned something about a sick cow.

Dolan was happy for Cord and Caitlyn in a sort of sadistic way. Their happiness meant he had no chance with the esteemed daughter of a racing mogul, but then again he never did. In reality it wasn't the woman as much as the thought of having someone love him as she did Cord. He wanted a woman like that.

How wimpy did that make him sound?

He tossed the pillow aside and it rolled to the floor. "Great." Fingers grasping the edge of the sheet, he tore the covers from his naked body. Running a palm over his face, he scooted to the edge of the bed and pushed to his feet. Thoughts of the redhead from last night materialized as he bent to retrieve the pillow. She had been the only ray of sunshine yesterday—and that voice.

Deep. Sexy.

A series of tingles erupted in his cock. He reached down and gave his balls a scratch. Damned if the memory of her didn't make him hard. He could have sworn there was something between them, a connection, when she turned and smiled at him. What he'd give to fall asleep each night listening to the sensual cadence of her voice whispering in his ear.

"Shit. You could have at least gotten her name." But there hadn't been time. Time was a precious commodity for a foundering horse. Yet in this case Travis Wood had overreacted. Thankfully the mare hadn't digested enough oats or grain to cause her permanent damage. Even still, Dolan had promised the boy he'd stop by this morning.

He padded across the cool marble floor toward the master bathroom. After finishing up at the Wood's last night, Dolan had considered swinging by Jester's, but it had been too late and he had been too tired. The chances that the woman was still there were slim. A prize catch like her wouldn't stay unattached for long. Of course nothing was holding him back from stopping by his friend's house tonight and getting the 411 on Red.

Who knew? Maybe she was the answer to his lonely existence.

Inhaling a ragged breath, he almost choked on his unexpected chuckle. At twenty-eight he had his whole life ahead of him. Pulling the door open, he stepped into the bathroom. It wasn't large, but comfortable. Two sinks, a bathtub, closed-in shower, and of course a commode tucked away behind another door. He passed through it to relieve himself. As he placed his palm against the wall to brace himself, he continued to analyze why the hell he felt so despondent these last couple of weeks.

Maybe it was the fact that he had never really had a family. At ten he had lost both parents in an avalanche during a skiing trip. Cord's father had taken him in, raised him like a son, but it hadn't been the same. Now Uncle Cordell was gone. Cord was married, completely enraptured in Caitlyn.

Dolan sighed.

With a final shake he finished up, flushed and headed toward the shower. The glass door squeaked as he opened it. Adjusting the knobs, he jutted his hand beneath the flow to check the temperature. Too cold. He gave the knobs another twist. When the water was hot enough he stepped inside, pulling the door close.

Steam rose bathing him in its warmth. For a moment, he allowed the water to pound his face.

Visions of the redhead who captivated him last night still lingered in the back of his mind. He had fallen asleep to the heat of turquoise eyes and a come-and-get-me expression forever engraved into his memory.

Oh yeah. He could have lain in bed forever with the image of her hips swaying to the seductive music haunting his consciousness. With just a smile the temptress had bewitched him. Damned if he couldn't smell her sweet powdery scent.

He reached for the soap and began to suds his body. For some reason his skin felt sensitive, nerve endings close to the surface making him aware of his callused hands moving leisurely to cleanse him.

What would her caress feel like against his skin, timid and shy or confident and bold—daring?

The thought of her fingers closing around his cock made him reach down and take hold of himself. With slow, measured pumps from base to tip, he thought of her, remembering the lacy garter, legs long enough to wrap around his waist, and a heart-shaped ass just begging for his attention.

He didn't think it was possible but his cock grew firmer, his balls drawing close to his body. His grip tightened. He sucked in a sharp breath before easing back against the cold tile of the shower. Once, twice, he pumped his hand up and down, sending tingles of sensation down his erection.

It felt good—damn good, but he would rather a certain redhead be beside him stroking and kissing every inch of his body.

Harder and faster, he thrust his hips forward, pushing his engorged erection through his fingers. All the time he thought of her hands on him. His free palm pressed against the wall. His knees locked as he eased in and out of his grasp over and over. Pre-come, warm and wet, met his touch as he slid his hand over the crown sending a tremor throughout his body.

What would it feel like to have those full lips replacing his hand?

An image of her naked, her skin slick from the falling water, materialized in his head. From down on her knees, she looked up at him. Blood slammed into his testicles creating sweet pain that curled his toes. Damn if he could almost feel her touch against his thighs as she wrapped her beautiful mouth around his cock.

He uttered a moan of pleasure stilling his hand briefly to savor the feel and make the image last longer.

Would she hesitate or relish his masculine flavor and drink from his essence? Better yet, what would she taste like if they changed positions? What if he spread her thighs wide and sucked her clit deep into his mouth?

Another tremor shook him to the core. Increasing the pace, he pumped unsteady strokes up and down.

Feels— He sucked in a breath and released it —*so good.*

His climax climbed higher and higher, erupting with a force that shook him. Lights burst behind his eyelids as lightning ripped down his shaft. He didn't even try to restrain the cry upon his lips. The sound of ecstasy felt like it was ripped from his diaphragm.

Shit. He'd completely forgotten about Rowdy.

Dolan's knees almost gave with the restraint it took to remain quiet. Breathless, heart pounding, he stood listlessly listening for any telltale signs his friend was awake. Seconds past, but the only sound was the water beating against the glass like raindrops against a window. That's when he made up his mind. He had to find her—had to know why he couldn't get her off his mind.

How long he leaned against the wall he didn't know. Pulling himself together, he finished soaping and rinsing his body and hair. It was time to get to work.

Switching off the water, he opened the door and retrieved a towel. Quickly he dried off and then ran it briskly over his hair, finger-combing it as he stepped out of the shower. The mirror was fogged with condensation. He made a swipe across the glass and stared into sorrowful eyes he didn't recognize.

"Enough," he grumbled. "Your pity-party has come to end." He turned away from his reflection determined to have a good day—an even better night.

The fresh scent of soap and woodsy aftershave tickled

Tracy's nose. She fought the sneeze threatening to interrupt Travis Wood Senior as he pointed out the features of his stables.

"Twelve stalls. We're not very large in comparison to the others here in town, but we're clean." She could see pride in his serious eyes as well as the confident way he held himself. Head high, shoulders back, each step taken with determination behind it. He stroked his large hand down his handlebar mustache. Late forties, he wasn't a bad looking man, honed by hard work. One thing she knew without a doubt, he was a no-nonsense man.

Every stainless steel rail was polished until it shined. The walkway was swept and probably mopped instead of sprayed because there was no standing water. Half of the stalls were occupied with horses happily munching on hay and oats. A sorrel with three white socks neighed. Another horse answered back clawing the ground.

"Our stock is healthy and of acceptable lineage," he stated matter-of-factly.

She flashed him a genuine smile. "I can see that."

Her Uncle Carl had called in a favor. Wood hadn't warmly welcomed her, but she would take what she could. Winning him over would be easy. Not because she had long legs and a voice that seemed to mesmerize men, but she was good at her job—damn good.

"Easy girl." The soft voice of a young man rose from a stall ten feet away.

"My son, Travis Junior," Wood announced. A gleam sparked, replacing his seriousness. That was, until the teenager stepped out of the stall. He wore no hat like his father's expensive Stetson and that wasn't the only difference. Where Wood Senior's clothes were clean and pressed, down to the

30

front seam of his jeans, his son looked in disarray. Straw and dirt dotted his wrinkled shirt half tucked in and half out of his jeans. His boots were scuffed and there was weariness on his taut features that seemed to grow even tighter when his gaze met his father's.

Wood Senior frowned. "What the hell—" He glanced sheepishly at Tracy. "Sorry ma'am." His expression hardened as he turned back to his son. "What's going on here, boy? Looks like you slept in those clothes."

Travis immediately started to brush off his jeans. "Uh... I did." He fidgeted, clearly looking for an answer. "I—I mean, yeah, I fell asleep out here last night."

The look on Wood's face said he wasn't buying his son's lie, but he held his tongue. Instead he said, "Come meet our new vet."

"Vet?" Travis's voice cracked as he stared at the stethoscope around her neck and the black bag she carried. He stole a quick glance toward the mare in the stall. The telltale sign that something was afoot caught Tracy's interest. The straw had been beaten down and the mare seemed lethargic. "What about Crane?"

Ahhh... The infamous Dolan Crane.

Her young cousin had given her the scoop on the other vets in the area, including the one that made all the women in town lust after him. Laurie had sighed as she described the man's handsomeness and his reputation as a playboy.

Tracy had almost swallowed her tongue when her cousin cupped a hand over her mouth and whispered, "Rumors are he likes ménages." Flush faced, the girl had giggled while Tracy had felt a spark of interest, one she had extinguished immediately.

She wasn't looking forward to meeting this playboy vet. He

31

wouldn't be receptive to her encroaching on his territory, she was sure of that. The Woods had been his customers until now.

"Tracy Marx," Wood Senior introduced. "I'll deal with Crane."

Travis jutted his hand out. "Pleasure to meet you, ma'am." He shot another look toward the mare and then wiped his palms on his jeans.

Not if your troubled expression means what I think it does. She didn't speak her mind but thought it better to check the mare as soon as possible. "The pleasure is mine."

"Deal with me, how?" came a deep smooth voice from behind her.

Color drained from Travis's face and Wood Senior's expression grew taut.

She pivoted on the toe of her boot, almost toppling over when her breath caught.

The dark stranger from last night stood approximately twenty feet away. Their eyes met. Sparks flew between them thickening the air so that the next breath was difficult to inhale. Her pulse leaped and warmth sizzled through her veins.

For a moment, he appeared overtaken as well. That was until the sexy grin he wore faded. His brows furrowed as if he struggled to understand the situation. Then his gaze dropped to her chest.

Now that was embarrassing. Heat flashed across her cheeks. She looked down to see if the buttons of her cotton shirt were open, but only saw the stethoscope hanging between her breasts. She glanced back up at him. That's when Tracy saw the stethoscope around his neck and the matching black bag in his hand.

Oh shit! Every ounce of confidence fled from her body. Her

mystery man was her competition.

Dolan Crane.

She swallowed hard. Fate must be having a fuckin' good laugh at her. The first man who had ever made her body react with such unadulterated lust was the one she hoped to squeeze out of business.

With determination in his step he marched up to her and extended his hand. "Dolan Crane."

Their palms met. Electricity zinged through her. "Tracy Marx," she mumbled, trying to retract her hand, but he held on.

"What's going on here?" She knew his question was targeted toward Wood even though his dark eyes seem to burn a hole through her.

"Had plans to call you today," Wood said while his son flashed Crane a helpless look.

Tracy jerked her hand in vain as his fingers tighten around hers. Controlled strength surrounded her like a glove.

He stepped closer.

If he was trying to intimidate her, it was working. It felt like an army of ants crawled across her flesh to raise goose bumps. She almost jumped out of her skin when his tone deepened. "What about?" There was a growl in his voice. Amazingly, she was aware of the heat of his body, the way his spicy cologne grew stronger as the fire in his eyes flamed brighter. His cock filled out the front of those jeans in a way that clouded her senses. The T-shirt stretched tight over strained muscles didn't help.

"Miss Marx is a vet," Travis's voice strained before his father could respond.

"Kind of drew that assumption on my own." He focused his full attention on Wood, while keeping her within his grasp.

33

"Wood?"

Travis Senior tore off his hat and ran his fingers through his hair. "Well it's like this, Crane. Doc Zimmerman is due to retire soon—"

"Yes."

"You can't blame a man for looking out for his investments." A hint of frustration rose in Wood's voice.

"Any problem with my work? Any cause to look elsewhere?" Clearly Crane wasn't backing down without a fight.

"My hand." Tracy finally spoke up. Crane faced her once again. She raised a single brow. "Could I have my hand back? I need to get to work."

His nostrils flared. He seemed to hold on to her longer before letting go just to show her that he was in control.

Her heart lunged into her throat. Damned if she didn't find that sexy as well. Still she had to stand her ground. She wouldn't let Crane chase her out of California. This was her opportunity for a new start.

"Look I know this is awkward, but we're professionals. It's the way things are." Well, bravo to her for speaking up and not really saying anything of real value. She wiped her now sweaty palm on her jeans. "I mean this town is big enough for the two of us."

Oh God. I can't believe I said that. Her words painted an image of a showdown in an old Western movie. By the simmering heat in his eyes he might just pull a six-gun and blow her away.

He gave her one of those you've-got-to-be-kidding looks and then turned to the two men beside her. "Travis. Wood." A nod followed the brisk run of his fingers along the brim of his hat. "Miss Marx." Without another word he turned and walked away.

Whoosh, she mentally brushed her brow. Dodged that bullet, but she still had to win over Wood who was frowning, which told her that Crane was a decent vet he hated to lose. Tracy knew she'd get past that issue. Of course, there was that other problem.

The attraction she felt for one hot cowboy who despised her.

Hey wait—

Anger began to rise. It crawled up her neck stinging her ears. Crane had referred to her as Miss Marx—not Dr. Marx. Was it a faux pas or an intentional act of disrespect? Either way his lack of acknowledgement stung and it made her madder than hell.

"So it begins," she hissed beneath her breath.

Chapter Three

Heavy footsteps carried Dolan to his truck. With more strength than required he swung the door open, tossed his bag on the seat and slammed the door after he got inside. Jaws clenched, he released the breath he hadn't known he held. In mere seconds he'd lost a customer and the chance with the woman of his dreams, or was it more like a nightmare?

"Shit." Ripping his hat off his head, he tossed it on the passenger seat.

She was a goddamn vet. The sexy redhead was his competition.

Didn't that beat all? That's all he needed, especially after yesterday's screwed-up day.

Twisting the key he started the truck, holding on too long so that the ignition wound tight. "Fuck." His palm slammed against the steering wheel. "A goddamn vet," he repeated shaking his head. With one shove, he crammed the vehicle into gear and pressed the accelerator. Tires screeched. Gravel popped. He was out of there.

As telephone poles blurred by him, his fingers tightened around the steering wheel. "Well, buddy, good thing you didn't pick her up last night."

How disastrous would that have been?

The irony of the situation was almost laughable. He could imagine the morning-after talk between them when they discovered who the other was, or had she already known who he was? He sure as hell hadn't expected her presence in town.

"Not the end of the world." He tried to convince himself. He would win on his merits. There was no denying it. He was a good vet. Plus, he had already begun to establish himself with Doc Zimmerman and his customers.

Dolan looked over the acres and acres of green pastures.

On the other hand, the men he had dealt with in the racing arena were a horny bunch. Tracy Marx had looks, a killer body and that damn sexy voice.

"I'm screwed," he groaned, pulling off onto a side road heading for his cousin's ranch.

Cattle grazed and a handful of horses was visible from the road as he pulled his truck to a stop before a big red barn. Cord leaned against a corral watching the pride of his ranch, Mystery Walker, prance along the fence line.

His cousin had the Midas touch.

After winning the two-year-old colt sired by Empire Maker, the 2003 Belmont winner, in a poker game, he went on to steal the heart of Caitlyn Culver who was now Mrs. Daily. The two of them had slipped away to Las Vegas and gotten hitched recently.

Grabbing his bag, Dolan climbed out of the truck. The screen door of the house squeaked and his cousin's new bride emerged. The tall brunette with eyes the color of the California sky literally ran into her husband's waiting arms. Their happiness squeezed Dolan's chest. For some godforsaken reason the image of one redhead veterinarian filled his head.

"Man, you've got shit for brains." He shook the image from his head and headed over to the couple.

"Dolan," Cait screamed, releasing Cord to circle her arms around his neck. She pressed her lips against his cheek as he embraced her.

Closing his eyes, he inhaled deeply, almost laughing. Instead of the familiar scent of perfume she smelled of bacon. He opened his eyes, burying his nose into her sweet smelling hair. "Mmmm... You smell good enough to eat."

Sweet laughter touched his ears as she gave him a playful shove. "I've cooked breakfast." Pride laced her tone, as well as the ear-to-ear grin she wore announcing she was pleased with herself. The pampered princess had gone from being waited upon to cooking and cleaning house. It took a lot of work to keep up a cattle ranch.

Cord took a step forward. "Remember that's my wife." There was a smile on his face, but Dolan could see the unease in his gaze.

"Haven't forgotten, cuz." Dolan stepped out of Cait's arms, putting distance between them. "Just couldn't resist a little sugar in the morning," he said jokingly, but the truth was he found a little comfort in her touch.

Cord didn't have a thing to worry about, but that didn't stop him from taking possession of his wife. They were family. Besides Cait was madly in love with her husband and Dolan didn't pursue married women. No matter what others thought of him, he did have some scruples. He might push the envelope when it came to sex, but he respected another man's woman.

Of course, if a couple invited him to play, who was he to turn them down? There was nothing like watching the ecstasy on a woman's face while two men drove her out of her mind.

Truth was that sometimes a man got too caught up in his own pleasure to savor that of the woman. Personally, he lived to hear a woman's breathy cries, to see the softness of her face harden, her screams of rapture as she shattered in his arms, and then the quiet bliss that followed.

That's what made a man a man.

In fact, he prided himself on making sure each woman who left his bed was satisfied, but left wanting more of what he had to offer. Given the opportunity, he'd turn that sexy little veterinarian every which way but loose.

"Dolan?" Cait pulled her brows together.

He blinked realizing he must have zoned out. "Yes," he answered to find both of them staring at him with concern. "Sorry. Lot's on my mind." The heavy sigh he released didn't help.

"You okay?" Cord's grip tightened on Cait. She cocked her head as confusion tugged on her brows, but she didn't resist his hold.

Dolan jerked off his hat and ran his fingers through his hair. "Lost a colt yesterday. To top it off there's a new vet in town."

"Yikes. Sorry."

He squared his hat on his head. "Thanks."

"Breakfast?" Cait asked.

"Little minx wants to show off her culinary abilities with bacon and eggs." Cord kissed the tip of her nose.

"Thanks, but no thanks. I've got a full schedule." Besides he needed to stay one step ahead of the redhead nipping at his heels. "Cow in the barn?" From what Cord had told him earlier about the young cow it sounded as if she had mastitis, an inflammation of the udder.

"Yeah," Cord replied as they headed for the barn. "So what's this new vet like?"

"Female," Dolan said dryly.

Cord pulled to halt before the opened double doors. His eyes widened. "The hell you say?"

Dolan nodded. "Yep. Redhead."

"Good looking?" Cait gave her husband a playful slap against the arm for the question as she entered.

"Yep." Dolan stepped inside. The scent of hay tickled his nose.

"So when do we get to meet her?" Cait asked.

Meet her? Dolan was confused. Why would they want to meet her? "Never."

"Never?" Both Cait and Cord said in chorus.

"Not my type," he lied. Besides he needed to find some way to run the little redhead out of his city.

Tracy's next stop was the Laski ranch. It was a quaint little place, ten acres with a small stable and Spanish manor. Uncle Carl had made a telephone call and Kevin Laski had agreed to speak with her.

It was more like check her out. He had yet to take his eyes off her breasts. As they headed for the stables, he hesitated. She stopped and looked over her shoulder. Without the slightest hint of decorum he caressed her ass with his slimy gaze.

This sucks, she thought. If she were a man this would never happen.

"Had some problems with this horse." He pointed to a gelding a rider was brushing down after an obvious vigorous workout. Sweat blanketed the horse's coat. His nostrils flared as he breathed heavily. He clawed the ground nervously. "Think you can tell me what his issue is?"

Oh goody—a test. She should have seen this one coming.

Keeping a rein on her temper, she strolled up to the horse and set her bag on the ground. For a while she just watched the animal, noting his rapid respiration by the way his flanks swayed in and out. The animal's nostrils were a brighter red than normal. Red lines at the side of the eyes were evident. Placing her fingertips against the horse's lower jaw, she gently pressed the facial artery to the inner surface of the jaw bone below the heavy cheek muscles. His pulse sped out of control.

She glanced back at Laski only to find his gaze plastered on her jean-covered ass again. He didn't even have the good sense to appear embarrassed.

"Without further testing and examination I believe your horse has EIPH." She wiped her hands on a towel the rider handed her. "Thank you." She returned the towel.

"EIPH?" Laski feigned ignorance, but the gleam in his eyes gave him away. The rider hid a grin behind his hand. Add insult to injury, even the horse made a snickering sound.

Okay. She'd play along.

"Exercise-Induced Pulmonary Hemorrhage, commonly known as bleeding." She couldn't believe he thought so little of a woman's ability. "Seventy—"

He glanced over her shoulder and she turned to see what caught his attention as well as the rider's.

Crap. Tracy's backbone stiffened. She barely held back a huff of exasperation. This couldn't be happening again.

Heading straight for them was none other than Dolan Crane. He wore the same scowl she had seen on his handsome face earlier, only this time his footsteps pounded the sidewalk. He didn't even try to hide his displeasure.

Forget him and focus. What had she been saying?

"Uhhh..." *Oh yeah.* "Seventy to hundred percent of horses in racing and training experience EIPH, which you already knew," she added just to let Laski know she was aware of his intentions.

A bushy brow rose, and then he brushed her off as easily as dust off his sleeve. He turned to welcome his guest.

God. She wanted to slap that shit-eating grin off the man's face as he shook Crane's hand. Then both of them narrowed their gazes on her.

Stay cool. She inhaled a breath of confidence, determined not to let either man get the best of her.

"Dr. Crane," she acknowledged him before she continued to speak to Laski. "Which also means that you know the American Association of Equine Practitioners recommends a horse be declared ineligible to race for a minimum of ten days after the first incident, second incident twenty days." What infuriated her was the damn man knew what was wrong with the animal and still had him exercised to the point of bleeding.

The idiot should be shot.

She also bet he had scheduled this awkward meeting between her and Crane—the conniving sonofabitch.

Beneath the rim of his hat, Crane kept his dark gaze pinned on her, making her as nervous as a fish in a blender. She licked her lips and his attention went immediately to her mouth. The stinging sensation as her nipples grew taut was all she needed.

What was it about this man that made her body squirm with desire? She crossed her arms over her chest. The action made her lacy bra scrape across her sensitive nubs. A burn started low in her belly.

This is ridiculous, she mentally chastised.

"Hmmm..." Laski nodded like one of those dog thingies perched on a dashboard. "Smart and pretty. Dangerous combination wouldn't you say, Crane?"

"Extremely," Crane replied, before turning his hot glare on Laski. "What I don't understand is why my orders were not followed." The veins in his neck bulged. He was pissed and this time it wasn't directed her way.

Yippee!

"I explained the importance of using the patches every day for ten days to bring down Dunguard's blood pressure." He reached out and gently stroked the horse's neck. "You can't continue to run this animal without being prepared for the consequences. One too many times and you'll kill him."

Bravo. Chew his ass good.

Maybe Crane wasn't so bad after all.

Tracy flinched as he suddenly turned his steely glare on her. "Now let's talk about her. Looking to replace me?"

Gulp! Her eyes widened. Erase her last thought.

"Absolutely not," Laski said. "Just doing Carl a favor by letting his niece visit today."

Visit? How humiliating. Heat flooded her face as her arms unfolded.

"Favor." Red-hot anger roared to the surface before she could restrain it. "You call watching my ass for the last thirty minutes a favor? If you had no intention of giving me a chance, why the hell did you even agree to meeting me?" She didn't wait for an answer. She turned to Crane and growled, "And you—"

Dammit. She braced her hands on her hips to hide the tremor that shook her, but it didn't work. She couldn't stop trembling.

"—get over yourself," she said, more sharply than she intended. "This isn't personal." There was so much more she wanted to say but couldn't get past the man's haunting eyes. It was like falling into the dark abyss leaving her speechless.

Damn him. Damn him to hell.

It took all the strength she had to tear her gaze away from him. When she did she bent and retrieved her bag. Tears swelled in her eyes, but she refused to let them fall. Without another word she turned and walked away.

Dolan Crane would not run her out of town. If anything, he would be the one leaving.

Chapter Four

Dolan eased back in the booth and tried to relax, but the fire he had seen in Dr. Marx's eyes earlier today was burned into his memory. Not only had she put Laski in his place, she'd managed to do the same to him.

It chapped his ass to know she was right. Soliciting his clients wasn't personal, but it sure as hell felt like it. Wrapping his fingers around a cold glass of beer, he took a long drink and let the amber wash away his thirst.

"Gotta love Hooters," Rowdy said, grinning. His hungry gaze slid up the backside of a long-legged brunette as she bent over to pick up a fork off the floor. "Beer. Burgers. And good looking women."

Dolan had to agree. In fact, he had made the restaurant selection thinking the scenery would chase a certain fiery redhead from his mind. The jukebox flipped to another song and the rocking beat of Keith Urban singing "You look good in my shirt" conjured an image of the redheaded vet in Dolan's bedroom standing sexy in one of his T-shirts.

Clearly his plan wasn't working—not by a long shot.

Had there been tears in her eyes as she had turned away from him? For some silly reason the thought weighed heavy on him. Dammit. Hurting her wasn't what he aimed to accomplish. He just wanted her gone and even that wasn't true. Screw seeing her in his T-shirt. What he really wanted was her naked and in his bed.

There. He'd said it. He had the fuckin' hots for the woman who could damage his career.

"Hungry?" He glanced up at a large-breasted blonde whose nametag identified her as Alyssa. She was new here. Through half-shuttered eyes, she looked down at him, giving him the distinct impression she wasn't speaking of the burger and fries she set down before him. To make it even clearer in his mind she leaned forward and reached across the table to retrieve the ketchup.

Nice breasts. Rowdy joined him in taking a good look.

"Ketchup?" She eased into a standing position, making sure he saw every bit of what she had to offer.

He winked, taking the bottle from her hand. "Thank you."

Alyssa smiled prettily, placing a slip of paper beneath his napkin. "The pleasure is mine." She turned and quietly walked away.

Might just give her a call tonight, he thought with less enthusiasm than usual. That alone told him his head wasn't where it should be. His stomach growled as if confirming the fact. He gave the ketchup lid a twist and tipped it over.

Rowdy cocked his head to steal a glimpse at Alyssa's ass covered in tight short-shorts as she headed for the kitchen. "Do you have that effect on all women?" He shoved a French fry into his mouth.

Dolan glanced at the waitress staring at him from across the room and noted that she wasn't as attractive as one redheaded veterinarian. Nor did she have a voice like silk. "Nah." He gave the ketchup bottle a couple quick shakes and a big blob of sauce plopped on his plate, splashing upon his shirt and arm. "Fuck." He grabbed a napkin and wiped his arm and then his shirt. This was gonna stain. Would anything be easy today?

Rowdy set his beer down. "Everything okay?"

The ketchup bottle wobbled as Dolan angrily placed it on the table. "That obvious?"

"Well. Yeah. What's up?" His friend picked up his hamburger.

"Lost a foal yesterday." Dolan hesitated. The colt's death still bothered him, but there was more to his unrest. "There's this woman," he heard himself admit.

"Don't tell me you're in love?" Amusement laced his friend's voice.

"Hell no." Dolan blurted the words and then calmed himself before he continued. "Just the opposite. Damn woman is my competition."

Rowdy stopped midway into taking a bite of his burger. "Competition?" He eased his sandwich upon the plate. "She's a veterinarian?" A shadow passed before his friend's eyes.

"Yeah." Dolan took another swig of his beer. "To top it off she's smart and sexy as hell. Flaming red hair."

Rowdy choked. "Red hair?" He looked a little peaked.

"You okay?"

His friend cleared his throat. "Sexy as in you're afraid that she'll romance your clients away or—" he studied Dolan, "—are you attracted to her?"

Both. Dolan pushed his fingers through his hair. "Business, of course." The lie stuck in his throat.

"Are you sure?" Rowdy pressed. "Looks like there might be something more."

"Shit. It's that obvious?" He was usually more discreet, but there was no denying there was something about this woman that consumed him.

His friend grinned, picking up his hamburger. He took a bite, chewed for a moment and then swallowed. "You know—" Grabbing his napkin, he wiped a big drop of mustard from the corner of his mouth. His eyes danced with mischief. "I've got this gal lined up for Monday night. I think you might like her. Why don't you join us?"

Why did he feel as if Rowdy was setting him up? "I don't know."

"Wow. Dolan Crane turning down an opportunity to get laid." He taunted him. "This woman must really be screwing with your head."

He had no idea.

"C'mon. You'd be helping me out. She has this fantasy." His friend took another bite of his hamburger. Chewing, he said, "Two men. Handcuffs." He swallowed before concluding, "I guarantee you'll love her."

Dolan thought for a moment. He needed a diversion. "What the hell. Why not?"

Another French fry disappeared into Rowdy's mouth. "Great. My house. Eight o'clock."

Dolan looked down at his shirt, remembering he had several more appointments before he could call it a night. "I'd better wipe this ketchup off before it stains." He got up from the table and headed for the bathroom.

"Hooters." Tracy huffed in disbelief. She couldn't believe her last client had recommended the place and she had taken it. It wasn't a place she particularly cared to have lunch, especially alone. At least she had the good sense to call ahead and order a chicken sandwich to go. She'd just eat the sandwich while heading to her next call. Pulling her truck into a parking space, she cut the engine and got out.

The cutest little brunette opened the heavy glass door and welcomed her. "Alone or meeting someone?"

"Alone. No. I mean to go. I called in an order," Tracy corrected, wondering why it always felt so pitiful entering a restaurant alone. As she stood at the hostess desk, she scanned the restaurant. Just what she thought, the majority of occupants were men ogling the waitresses. She frowned until her gaze landed on a familiar face. Rowdy sat alone in a booth.

"Your name?" the cheery waitress asked.

"Marx."

"Give me a second and I'll check on your order," the brunette offered before she turned to seat a couple who came through the door.

Tracy heaved the strap of her purse over a shoulder. Maybe she'd just say hello. As she approached, Rowdy got a huge smile on his face that disappeared almost as quickly as it appeared. He shot a nervous glance toward the bathroom.

So, you're here with someone.

"Hey." His eyes widened as she slide into the booth across from him.

"Hi." She hid the grin begging to be released as he began to squirm. "Wha'ya up to?" The untouched hamburger in front of her smelled good enough to eat.

Rowdy wasn't usually short of words, but he seemed particularly quiet at the moment. "Eating."

Whoever he was with sure liked ketchup, she noted. "Moved into your new place yet?" She searched for small talk.

"Not yet. Closing is Monday morning." He glanced toward the bathroom for the second time. Putting him out of his misery, she stood. Relief fell across his face. "We still on for that evening?"

It probably should have bothered her that he was here with someone else while making plans to sleep with her Monday, but for some reason it didn't. Although he was a good-looking man, there weren't any real feelings other than friendship. "Sure." Lord knows she needed something to get her mind off of one particular veterinarian.

"Hey, why don't you wear that cute little bustier you wore that second night. You know the one."

Oh yeah. She knew the one. He hadn't let her wear it for long.

"It should drive my friend as wild as it did me." He laughed as she felt heat flood her face. "You said you were game for anything."

Those were her words and it was her fantasy. Now if she had the guts to go through with it.

"Miss Marx." Tracy jerked around. The brunette waitress stood beside her. "Your order is ready."

Ohmygod. How much had the waitress heard?

"My order? Oh. Yes. My order." She almost dropped her purse as she scrambled to find her credit card. Meanwhile, Rowdy sat there with the biggest grin on his face.

"Are you, Tracy?"

She was going to kill him. Ignoring him, she handed the woman her credit card. When the waitress was out of earshot, she faced Rowdy again. "Bastard," she whispered with a chuckle.

"You look so pretty all red and embarrassed." He winked. "Are you game?"

"Ohhh," she growled, turning to walk away without another

word.

"Was that a yes?" he hollered, following it up with a stream of laughter.

Yes. Yes. Yes. But she wasn't giving him the satisfaction of hearing her say it.

Crap. Now he was imagining seeing the woman.

Dolan wiped his damp palms down his jeans as someone who looked a lot like Tracy Marx exited the restaurant.

Red hair.

Tight jeans.

The wet spot on his T-shirt was right over a nipple that grew taut. With each step he took the material scrapped over the sensitive nub, and that wasn't the only thing firming. If he didn't watch it he'd have a raging hard-on by the time he reached the table.

Dammit. He had to put an end to the fascination he had for this woman. Maybe Rowdy offered him the right opportunity. He slid into the booth. Guilt written all over his friend's face.

Dolan checked his lunch. Nope. No bite out of his hamburger. Fries all where he left them and his beer looked untouched. Must be his imagination once again running away.

"We're on for Monday night. Anything I can bring?" he asked.

"Not a thing. I think I've taken care of everything." Rowdy looked away.

Odd.

"Need any help moving in?"

"Nah. I've hired a team of people to move and unpack me. I'll just sit back with a beer and supervise."

Dolan picked up his sandwich and took a bite. "Sounds like you have everything under control."

"I hope so." Rowdy chugged down his beer and then held up the empty glass to get the waitress's attention.

Alyssa didn't miss a beat. "Another round?" She batted long eyelashes at Dolan.

"Not for me." He took another bite of his hamburger, realizing how hungry he was. He'd skipped breakfast and the encounters with his competition this morning had left him more concerned about his livelihood than his stomach.

"I'll take another," Rowdy said.

"Are you sure?" She placed her palm on Dolan's shoulder and gave it a squeeze.

Surprisingly he felt nothing. Not a spark of interest, which was disconcerting. He loved women of all shapes and sizes. Every one of them held a mystery. They were like puzzles he prided himself on solving, but not today. Even the scent of her sweet perfume did nothing to him.

"I'll take another beer," Rowdy repeated.

"Can I get you anything else?" She drew a little circle on Dolan's shoulder.

The frustration on Rowdy's face was hard to miss. Dolan cleared his throat. "A beer for my friend."

She jerked her hand back, visibly bewildered by his lack of interest. "Of course." She faced Rowdy. "Can I get you anything else?"

"No, just the beer." As she turned to leave, Rowdy mumbled, "Thanks, buddy."

Dolan glanced at his watch, realizing the time. He pushed the last of his hamburger into his mouth. "I've gotta go. Anything planned for tonight?" He dug into his pocket and threw a twenty on the table before he rose.

Rowdy pushed his plate away from him. "Thought I'd hang out at Norton's. What about you?"

"Maybe. Depends on whether any emergencies arise. I'm on call this weekend, remember?"

Rowdy wagged his head. "Good enough. See you later."

"Later." He headed toward the exit.

As he got into his truck and turned the key, a wave of relief rose. His next client was female. Carissa Carter wouldn't be swayed by a sexy voice and long legs.

Chapter Five

The weekend flew by with amazing speed. The moving trucks had arrived late Saturday. Sunday had been a blur of unpacking box after box. Tracy was actually thankful to be away from all the paper, dust and work. A night on the town was just what she needed, plus she loved Chinese food. Leaning toward the mirror, she checked her makeup again. The scent of ginger wafted in the air drowning out the delectable aromas from the restaurant's kitchen. Fresh white lilies sat on the countertop reminding her of the ones in her own bathroom. She loved her new place. It was small, quaint and she couldn't wait for Sheldon to see it. The five-acre ranch would be a perfect place to raise a child.

Exhausted, she had almost cancelled when Rowdy called tonight. "Liar," she huffed to herself, picking her purse up from the bathroom sink. His promise to make the evening one she'd never forget had sharpened her curiosity. One more check in the mirror and she headed for the door. The fact she needed the touch of a man was the real reason she had agreed to dine with him tonight.

During dinner he had refused to tell her anything about his friend or the rest of the evening. She slung her purse over a shoulder and eased through the crowd noting how warm it was. After they finished dessert, she'd taken the opportunity to escape and regroup. A nervous wreck, she still couldn't believe she had agreed to a threesome. Her fortune cookie hadn't helped when she had read, "A dark stranger will change your life." Crane had haunted her thoughts since she had met him.

Arms slung along the back of the booth, Rowdy looked rather pleased with himself as she approached.

"What?" She slipped in next to him.

His arm folded around her. He pulled her to him so that they were chest to chest. His spicy cologne surrounded her reminding her of another man who wore similar cologne. His lips were so close they whispered across hers when he said, "God, you're gorgeous." Then he closed the distance between them. His kiss was everything she had remembered, firm yet gentle, coaxing as his tongue slid between her lips.

"Mmmm..." She leaned in for another caress.

It seemed strange, but Rowdy had been there to offer comfort after her divorce and now again as she fought to establish herself in this new city. Was he her guardian angel?

His palm skimmed the bare area between her silk shirt and slacks, sending goose bumps across her skin. "I can't wait to strip you naked. Taste you." He pressed his lips to her ear. "Ready to go?"

What was she thinking? Sensual words like his couldn't come from an angel. He was the devil in disguise. In fact, she was counting on him being as wicked as could be tonight.

"Yes." She sucked in a breath of anticipation as her breasts grew heavy and her nipples stung. There wasn't anything like the first signs of arousal.

He released her, reaching into his pocket to pull out a fifty. Lust simmered in his eyes as he placed the money on the table, grabbed his hat and put it on, before he scooted out of the booth. His features were tight as he extended her his hand.

55

Another series of tingles released moisture between her thighs. Her fingers closed around his, feeling the heat of his body.

Her pulse leaped. She didn't realize how much she needed to be made love to. There was a hunger inside her that had continued to build ever since she locked gazes with Crane at Jester's house Friday night. Just the thought of him took her need to a higher level. Tonight Rowdy and his friend would vanquish Crane from her thoughts for good.

A warm breeze blew from the south. Stars twinkled in the heavens as they walked into the night. Rowdy stopped several times in the dimly lit parking lot to steal a kiss. She laughed, loving his playfulness, while in the back of her mind she craved for the moment two men would cherish her body. A flood of excitement anointed her thighs. She was really going through with this.

As they reached his truck, he pressed her against the vehicle, his body trapping hers so that she felt his firm arousal hard against her belly. "Second thoughts?"

Her fingers curled into fists by her side as she resisted the urge to squirm against him. "Have you done this before?"

He nodded. The fire in his eyes burned even brighter. "It's like nothing you've ever experienced." He touched his nose to hers. His lips, feather-light, pressed to hers as he said, "Trust me." His minty breath was warm against her skin as he smoothed his mouth along her jaw line. "I promise," his voice dipped low, "we'll rock—your—world." The way he emphasized each word made her hot all over. Gently he brushed back a lock of her hair. His teeth scraped her earlobe, sending chills up her spine. "We'll leave no place on that beautiful body of yours untouched—unloved." A sexy growl followed that nearly undid her. "I can't wait to see you come apart in our arms." His tongue swirled around the shell of her ear.

Tracy's heart leaped into her throat. The picture he painted in her mind was exactly how she imagined it. Just once she wanted to do something forbidden, to feel as if she were the most desired woman in the world. Sandwiched between two men whose only focus was to drive her out of her friggin' mind. She inhaled a tight breath. Yes. That's what she wanted—a fantasy for one night.

As he took control of her mouth again, her hunger soared. She grasped his shirt, holding on. His tongue teased her lips before sliding between them to deepen the caress and break down any uncertainty that remained.

Nothing would dissuade her from the path she was on.

The kiss ended and instead of the blissful moment she expected, he glanced at his watch. "Shit. We've got to go." Grabbing her hand, he pulled her to the other side of the vehicle. A click sounded as he unlocked his truck, opened the passenger door and helped her inside. His actions were quick moving around the truck to get behind the wheel.

"In a hurry?" she chuckled as he crammed the key into the ignition.

"With you—always." He gave the key a twist and the engine roared to life.

"Such a liar."

Rowdy was artful when it came to foreplay. He knew what was required of a man to make a woman relax and put her into the mood. That's why she felt so comfortable with him. He didn't make her feel as if there was something wrong in seeking her pleasure with a stranger—hell, make that two.

"Did you bring that corset?"

She patted her purse. "Uh-huh." Inside was the corset along with a pair of stilettos, black stockings, and a lacy little thong. Of course, she wouldn't mention that she was thinking of one irritating veterinarian when she selected the ensemble.

"Great." He flashed a sexy grin. He accelerated and she held on for the ride.

Stopping before two elaborate wrought iron gates, he rolled down his window and punched in an access code. The gates moaned open. As they passed through the entrance and took a left, her anxiety rose again. He must have seen her uncertainty because he reached over and squeezed her hand.

"Here we are." He pulled into a driveway leading to a gorgeous two-story home of European influence. Large red brick gables, high-flowing, graceful roof lines and a fireplace with a decorative brick pattern along the front façade dashed her apprehension. Instead she breathed in the elegantly groomed landscape. Rich green grass and several topiary shrubs of leaping dolphins dotted the lawn around a fountain that disappeared from her sight as he steered his truck into a three car garage alongside a red two-door sports coup. The fact he lived in a gated community instead of a ranch revealed he lived a carefree lifestyle. The car screamed Rowdy was a playboy.

That's when Tracy realized she really didn't know much about him and nothing about his friend. Yet tonight she would lie in their arms. When tomorrow's light rose they would know each other intimately.

Tracy didn't wait for Rowdy to open her door. Nerves had her grabbing her purse and pushing the door open. She slipped out of the truck waiting beside it.

As he came around the vehicle, he winked and gathered her hand in his. Keys jingled as he selected the house key and unlocked the door. The garage opened up into a large utility room with a washer and dryer.

"It's not much, but I call it home." He ushered her through the dark room.

Reaching around her, he flipped the light switch. A flash of brilliance sparked and lights flooded the next room, stealing her sight for a second. As her vision returned, the first word that came to mind was "beautiful." The kitchen had an open brick oven, stainless steel conveniences, an island a cook would die for and the quaintest breakfast nook overlooking the backyard. She didn't have time to take in anything more as he grabbed her hand and escorted her into the family room.

Again she was taken aback. Rowdy's cowboy persona had her expecting a country living ambience, not the elegance that surrounded her. Mahogany trimmed the room with matching wood and leather furniture. An entertainment center adorned one entire wall. Surround sound, a sixty-four-inch, high-definition television and a selection of movies it would take Tracy several years to watch. As she took in the room, Rowdy released her hand and went directly to the bar, which was as much a masterpiece as some of the art hanging on the walls. Intricate carved wood with brass trim, marble countertop, and smoky glass gave it a look of grandeur.

"How did you accomplish all this in one day? I'm still not through unpacking."

"Movers and a decorator. Wine?" He reached for three glasses and a corkscrew.

"Uh. Sure." Rowdy's place was exquisite, but Tracy liked the country look and feel of her own house. After work she liked to kick her boots off and climb in the middle of the floor to play with Sheldon.

"Make yourself at home." Rowdy nodded toward an archway. "The bedroom is over there if you want to slip into something more comfortable." She didn't miss his devilish grin as he started to open the bottle.

Hugging her purse to her chest, she made her way to the

bedroom. The richness in this room was no different from the rest of his home. The centerpiece was a huge mahogany bed with bedposts that had to be eight feet tall. Even the fireplace was large and trimmed in reddish-brown wood. But the thing that caught her attention was the large tub visible from the bedroom. The thing was big enough to have a party in. Green vines with exotic colorful flowers circled the pillars that surrounded it making it look like an oasis.

Tracy placed her purse on the bed and then began to undress. Once again her anxiety rose, but she took a deep breath and pushed it aside. Instead she focused on loosening the laces on the corset. She slipped the black satin and red lace over her head and her nipples hardened, growing harder as the material scraped across them. She loved the way the garment cradled her breasts and hugged her ribcage. Goose bumps covered her arms as she stepped into the matching thong and pulled it up her hips.

Taking a seat on the bed, she carefully rolled a stocking up her leg. The silk was cool, stroking her skin to embrace her upper thigh. She took her time with the second stocking, briefly closing her eyes to savor the feel. The final touch to her ensemble was the black three-inch stilettos she inched her feet into. The click of heels against the marble floor was the only sound as she went into the bathroom.

A smile crept across her face. "Oh yeah." She gazed at her reflection in the full length mirror. "Sinful and naughty." Just the look she was going for. Voices from the other room made her twist around.

Rowdy's friend had arrived.

Dolan turned down the glass of wine Rowdy offered him for a shot of whiskey. The amber burned as it touched his throat. "Ahhh... Just what I needed." He slammed the shot glass on the bar and then pivoted. Not seeing the third individual in their intimate party he took the opportunity to survey his surroundings. As he walked the room, he said, "Not exactly what I expected, but nice."

His friend's taste had changed. Maybe it was the fact that with his current job he didn't have time for a ranch. Still, ranching was in a man's blood—once there it was hard to make a break. Truth was ranching didn't pay much and evidently computer programming did by the looks of his friend's place.

Nothing could beat the picturesque view of horses or cattle grazing and the freedom open land offered. The scent of hay was something Dolan had always loved. His home sat on the fringes of Cord's ranch. When Uncle Cordell passed, his cousin had gifted him with twenty acres and the small three-bedroom ranch house upon it to keep him near because the two of them were the last of their family. Dolan was a proud man. It had been hard to accept Cord's offer, but he too wanted to stay close.

"So, where is she?" He wanted to get this party started. The last couple days had been hellish. Not to mention, he hadn't seen his little redheaded veterinarian anywhere, which bothered him more than he cared to admit. Guess it was too much to hope that she'd gone back from where she came.

Before Rowdy answered, the bedroom door opened.

In one fell swoop the air in the room disappeared leaving Dolan dizzy. As if his thoughts had conjured the woman, Tracy Marx stepped into the room not more than four feet away.

Her eyes widened. Her jaw dropped. Shocked didn't describe the look of surprise on her face as their eyes met.

He shared her disquiet. Speechless, his feet rooted to the floor, the only thing that appeared to be working was his cock. The damn thing sprung to life.

Sexy didn't begin to describe how she was dressed. Stilettos and long legs wrapped in sheer black stockings led to narrow hips barely concealed by a thong. But it was the corset raising her breasts and presenting them as if they were dessert that almost gave him a heart attack. Wild red hair framed her face making her the most sensual creature he had ever laid eyes on. Not to mention, her soft female musk taunted him unmercifully.

Lust rumbled in his throat. He felt his nostrils flare. Tingles exploded in the center of his palms giving him the uncontrollable urge to bury his hands in her silky mass.

Her mouth snapped shut drawing into a thin line. She blinked hard before her gaze shot to their host. "Rowdy?" There was a quiver in her voice. Her fingers now balled into fists.

"What?" The lack of innocence in his friend's voice made Dolan turn and glare at him. "You two know each other?" Before either of them could comment, he said, "That's great. Makes getting to know each other easier."

"Easier," she repeated with enough heat in her tone to light a fuse. She faced Dolan with accusation in her eyes. Her palms now perched on her hips. "You set this up to humiliate me."

What the fuck was she talking about? "Humiliate you?" His voice was coarse as sandpaper as he closed the distance between them. Nose to nose, he huffed, "Woman, I want you gone—not in my bed." It was a bold-faced lie. He did want her in his bed, so badly he felt his control slipping.

She flinched at his cruel words. Color heated her cheeks. For a second the hardness in her features crumbled and moisture filled her eyes making them pools of blue.

Dammit. He didn't mean to hurt her. It just—

Before he could apologize, her backbone stiffened. Moist eyelashes batted her emotion away, almost as if it never existed and replaced it with one of pure disdain.

"Feeling is mutual." She whipped around, took several hurried steps and then drew to an abrupt halt. As if she second guessed her move, she pivoted again and walked back so that they were a foot away. With a toss of her head she sent her mass of red hair over a shoulder. "You know, Crane, you remind me of the first animal I treated." She narrowed her gaze. "He was a jackass, too." She was still hissing the insult when he reached for her.

The impact of their bodies coming together forced an indelicate "Ugh" from her. Chest to chest, hips to hips, he trapped her in his embrace.

Fury flickered in her eyes, dilating them. "Release me." Her heated breath washed over his face.

Release her? The hell he would. Instead he lowered his head and captured her stubborn mouth with his. The kiss was slow, hot, and he made sure thorough and unforgettable.

Taken unaware, she froze.

There was a second where time stood still and a thousand sensations seduced him. With a need that bordered on insanity he stroked her tender lips, savoring her essence and the softness of her skin.

Yes. The word hummed throughout him. He knew she would taste of heaven and hell.

She bit his lip.

"Fuck," he yelped, but didn't let her go as she attempted to shove him away. So much for making the damn kiss unforgettable.

The growl of frustration she released only ignited his need to devour her more. Their eyes met in a fiery exchange. A squeal came from her parted lips as he stepped forward, pinning her against the wall.

Her breathing was rapid, chest heaving to mimic his. Determination to resist him was etched on her brows. No way would she win in this game of wills. Before the night was over she would be melting in his arms.

"Dolan." He heard Rowdy's warning tone but ignored him to press his mouth to hers once again. In the exchange their teeth clashed.

She continued to struggle against his assault, but that didn't deter him. In reality he didn't know if he could stop. He had to taste her—all of her. Never had he wanted anyone like he did her. Since seeing her at Jester's she was all he could think of. She dogged his every waking moment and haunted his dreams.

He inhaled her powdery perfume and caressed the silkiness of her skin as he slid his palms down her body. Looping his hands behind her knees, he raised her to part her thighs and move between them. He fit so damn perfect, like he belonged there.

His hands traveled down her back and settled on her ass, cupping and squeezing, pushing her against his groin. As he grinded his hips into the sweet spot he hoped to be revealing soon, she tossed back her head and cried out. The delicate sound caught somewhere between passion and desperation. He prayed it was more of the first than the latter. Even still, he stroked her lips with his tongue urging her to give in, allow him to carry her to ecstasy.

But the time wasn't right. She continued to resist him.

Relentless with his kisses, he nibbled on her bottom lip, sucking it into his mouth. All the while, he caressed and rubbed against her body, tempting and teasing to break down her defenses.

Dolan knew the moment she surrendered. She sighed,

softening against him. Struggle gone, she crossed her legs at the ankles to hold him closer. Her mouth opened, welcoming him with an urgency to match his own. Knocking his hat off, she threaded her fingers through his hair, pulling him nearer to take the initiative and deepen the caress.

The touch of her tongue against his ignited an explosion of fire and ice. Male pride surged through his veins as he wrapped his arms possessively around her.

Damn. Her submission was even better than he had imagined. One after the other he swallowed her mewling cries.

Rowdy nudged him. "My turn." Dolan didn't want to let her go.

"Mine," he growled against her lips. Eyelids half-shuttered, she looked at him with such hunger that he swore he felt the tug. A shiver slithered up his spine.

"Ours," his friend insisted. "You've had her long enough. It's my turn."

Dolan wouldn't have released her, but she unfolded her legs and eased down his body to stand on her feet. She placed her palms on his chest and looked into his eyes to send his heart reeling. What was it about this woman that made his chest tighten—made it hard to breathe?

The calm she wore quickly began to crumble as she took a shuddering breath. "Rowdy," she whimpered.

Dolan stepped aside and his friend took his place.

Cupping her face, he hummed, "Hush, baby. Let us pleasure you."

"I don't think—"

Dolan watched as his friend stole her building objection with a heated kiss.

No way could Dolan let her leave. While Rowdy kept her

occupied, he inched between her and the wall. Brushing aside her hair, he began to caress her bare shoulder with his lips. Hands riding her hips, he slid his fingers forward to hug her flat abdomen.

Chapter Six

Tracy couldn't think clearly. Rowdy's mouth moved relentlessly over hers as he held her tight. She had waited a lifetime to experience something as explosive as what these two men offered. The battle between her and Dolan had been fucking hot, breaking down her resistance. Her surrender had rocked her. She knew immediately it was only a taste of what was to come. Tonight she would venture into the unknown. Discover what it felt like to step beyond the traditional lines of making love.

Crane stepped behind her, pressing his front to her back. Sandwiched between the softness of their cotton shirts and the stiffness of their jeans against her skin made her feel vulnerable. She inhaled their masculinity, hot and spicy.

Crane placed his hands on her waist and every bone in her body grew weak. The man's kisses had drugged her, but his touch was deadly. Wicked hands caressed her with reckless abandonment, stroking the bare flesh between her corset and thong. His fingertips set off a series of sparks across her skin every place they teased.

She was breathless when the kiss ended. Sucking in a much needed breath, she felt the trace of Rowdy's lips down her neck to the swell of her breasts. Rays of sensation burst in her nipples.

"Rowdy." His name was a mere whisper.

"*Shhh...* Darlin'." Crane's deep voice hummed in her ear. "Let us make you feel good."

She held her breath as his fingers traced the edge of her thong, high on her hips to the deep V close to the spot she was dying for him to touch. He slipped a finger beyond the elastic, gliding further, so dangerously close to her clit that she whimpered. A flood of desire dampened her thighs so quickly she squeezed them together to quiet the sudden ache.

"Relax." His finger grazed her sensitive nub.

Relax? Tracy nearly jumped out of her skin. Before she could pull herself together she felt a warm, wet tongue against her breast. With a nudge, her nipple popped out of its confines. Rowdy covered it with his mouth, gently sucking and teasing the distended peak with his teeth.

Oh God. Oh God. She needed to stop this insanity before it went any further.

"I—" She choked on the word before it morphed into a cry of pleasure. Baring her other breast, his sinful fingers began to squeeze and pinch the nipple. Her head fell back upon Crane's shoulder.

"I need to touch you," he growled, sending chills across her skin. His fingers danced through her pubic hairs moving so close to the pulse of her sex. "Do you want me to touch you?"

She groaned unable to restrain it. *Say no*, her mind screamed. She shouldn't—couldn't allow this to continue.

"So beautiful. Soft. Can I touch you?" He moaned, a low raspy sound that nearly undid her.

Every muscle in her body stiffened as she fought the growing lust that swept over her. *Just tell him no.* Instead she found herself knotted with anticipation, unable to refuse him, wanting what he offered and loving what Rowdy was doing to her breasts.

"Relax your thighs. Surrender and let me in." Crane barely grazed her clit and her legs widened like they were spring activated. His warm chuckle swept over her. "That's it, sweetheart."

The triumph in his voice should have infuriated her, but she didn't have time to react. A single finger parted her swollen folds and buried deep to rip the air from her lungs.

Her knees buckled. Heat swarmed her body. "Oh God," she breathed as he tightened his hold to keep her from falling. Achingly slow he thrust in and out of her pussy. She closed her eyes, imagining it was his cock. Another wave of moisture released. For a second her hips fell into the rhythm of his hand.

So good. So—

Her eyelids sprung wide. Out of nowhere a glimmer of sanity peeked beyond the haze her mind had become. What the hell was she doing?

She tensed and yanked away from Rowdy, grappling for her corset to shield herself. Her thighs snapped together trapping the hand between them. "I—"

Rowdy covered her mouth once again. Firmly he held her head, controlling the moment. Crane increased the pace down below, his thumb pressed on her clit and she lost it.

Throwing caution to the wind, she curled her fingers into Rowdy's shirt, angled her head and stabbed her tongue between his lips, mimicking the hand moving steadily between her legs. Spasms squeezed and released in her abdomen. Tingles burst like fireworks shooting into the sky. She bucked against Crane's hand once, twice, and then her orgasm roared to the surface shattering into a million pieces.

Rowdy swallowed her scream.

One after another, currents of ecstasy raced through her body, awakening every nerve. Flames flickered across her skin. Her pulse raced, heart beating out of control. A cry squeezed from between her lips.

"That's it, sweetheart." Crane slowed his pace. "Let it go." He focused his finger on the bundle of nerves and began a slow circular motion that was driving her to the edge of madness. Hitting a particular sensitive spot, her body jerked and another series of currents skyrocketed.

"Crane." Squirming beneath his touch, she cried out, "Please. No more." He retracted his hand and she slumped against him, sighing as her arms fell from around Rowdy's neck.

"Dolan." Crane wrapped his arms around her, snuggling his nose into her hair. "Call me Dolan. And, darlin', we've only begun to have our way with you."

To emphasize his friend's point Rowdy began to unlace her corset. She tried to stop him but he was quick, drawing the ribbon completely out of the garment. "Damn. Tracy." As he released the ribbon and let it join her corset lying at her feet, he admired her breasts. "Do you have any idea how beautiful you are when you're coming?" With a kick of his booted foot her corset slid across the room and out of her reach. "Dolan, you should have seen her." He brushed the underside of her breasts and then filled his palms with them. When he skimmed over her nipples a sting filtered through them bordering on pain and pleasure.

"Maybe I should go," she managed to say on a shuddering breath even as she leaned further into him.

Dolan's arms tightened around her. "Not on your life, sweetheart."

Why did it feel so natural to be held by this man? So right, yet so wrong. They were competitors. Nor should she forget the fact that he despised her. Well, outside the bedroom anyway.

"You can't leave now." Rowdy wove his fingers through her hair and pulled her mouth to his. "Please don't leave," he whispered against her lips.

Dolan turned her in his arms, forcing his friend to surrender her. Lightheaded, her mind spun, taking a moment for her senses to return. She'd nearly forgotten just how good looking he was. And those eyes, dark and mesmerizing, she could drown in them.

Without a word, he closed the distance between their mouths. This time his kiss was gentle, meant to seduce, and he was doing a damn good job. She leaned into him, opening her mouth when his tongue caressed between her lips.

Man, could he kiss.

Tracy savored his masculine flavor with a hint of whiskey. With one hand he held her head immobile, while his other palm slid down her body to cup the bare cheek of her ass. He squeezed, creating a flutter low in her belly. Bending his knees, he scooped his arms beneath her knees. She found herself cradled in his arms.

"Bedroom?" he asked, not taking his dark eyes off her face.

Rowdy darted around them and walked through the door she had left open. Dolan followed, his boots making a dull sound as they struck the floor.

Inside the room, he allowed her to slide down his frame. For a moment he held her close, and then he released her and stepped away. A cool breeze reminded her that she stood before him in only her thong, silk stockings and stilettos.

A moment of discomfort swarmed her as he reached for the hem of his T-shirt. As he pulled his shirt over his head, Tracy breathed in the sight of him. Broad and muscular, his washboard abs begged her to reach out and touch. It didn't help that the light covering of hair on his chest narrowed into a thin line that trailed down his firm stomach and disappeared into his jeans where an impressive bulge caught her eye.

Oh my, she thought but remained silent, unmoving.

"Come here." The dominance in his voice made her pulse leap and her feet move. As if they were on autopilot they carried her straight into his arms.

Their chests met, skin to skin. She gasped. Dolan's body heat bled into her as hundreds of goose bumps rose across her skin, even the dark ring around her nipples pimpled. The way he rubbed his torso against her was so sensual—so hot.

Now this was heaven.

"I'll take some of that." Rowdy stepped behind her. Dolan placed his hands on her arms as Rowdy cuddled close. Her eyes widened. The fact he, too, had taken off his T-shirt and she hadn't noticed surprised her. Yet she didn't miss the warmth of his chest moving erotically against her back or the nibble on her shoulder as his palms rested on her hips.

Tracy almost laughed. The apprehension she had experience earlier about being with these two men at once was gone. In fact, she was looking forward to the moment their bodies came together. Just the thought of them filling her made her wet, ready.

"Damn," Rowdy cursed, releasing her. She broke the gaze between her and Dolan and glanced over her shoulder. "Boots. Once I get started I don't plan on stopping." He wagged his brows playfully.

Dolan must have felt the same way because he stepped away and sat on the bed to take his boots off, too. Their absence left her feeling exposed. She crossed her arms over her bare chest.

"Don't hide those lovely breasts from us, darlin'." Dolan tossed a boot and sock aside. "You're breathtaking." The fire burning in his eyes confirmed his words.

She inhaled a breath, her nipples growing taut as she dropped her arms to her side. The creak of a nightstand drawer caught her attention and she looked just in time to see Rowdy extracting something from it. Hand hidden behind his back, he flashed a devilish grin, before he closed the drawer.

What was he up to?

She didn't have time to ponder the thought as Dolan approached on predatory steps that made her heart beat faster. She wanted him—knew she had to have him when he stopped several feet away.

His gaze fell from her face to her hips. "Thong. Off."

A demand—not a request.

His arrogance should have infuriated her, yet a flood of arousal was the result. Plus she loved the deep rumble in his throat when he revealed, "I need you naked." He paused, staring at her with a heat that shimmered over her skin. As if it were an afterthought, he added, "Leave the stockings and stilettos."

Not a thread of hesitation rose. She shoved her thumbs between the silky material and her hips when warm hands stopped hers. Glancing over her shoulder, Rowdy smiled. "Here." He nuzzled her neck. "Let me do it."

Achingly slow, he inched the thong down her hips, past her thighs and legs until the material circled her ankles. He nudged her foot and she raised it allowing him to remove the last of her clothing.

Tracy Marx was gorgeous.

Legs parted, standing in only stockings and heels, she looked like a succubus hell bent on seducing him. For a moment he wished he was Rowdy, smoothing his palms over her slender legs and across hips made for riding. But then he couldn't see the flaming curls at the apex of her thighs trimmed into the shape of a heart. Blood rushed his groin, forcing a groan through clenched teeth.

Dolan pulled in a tight breath as his friend cradled her succulent breasts. Firm and rounded, her breasts were an image of perfection. Just the right size—a handful, nothing wasted.

Rosy nipples hardened beneath his scrutiny, begging to be suckled, and he would. Before the night was over he would know her body and every spot that made her sigh or cry out in pleasure.

He raised his eyes to meet hers. Her breaths were broken pants of desire. "Touch me." Her request was so faint he thought he'd imagined it, but the excitement that surged through him was real.

Rowdy closed in on her nipples, moving them between his thumbs and forefingers. Her eyelids fell, dark lashes lying like small crescents upon her cheeks. She leaned back into him, an expression of pure bliss on her beautiful face as her mouth parted on a sigh.

He had the absurd urge to grin like a kid in a candy store, that is until he realized she'd been speaking to his friend—not him.

"Rowdy," she moaned.

Well shit.

As her breathing elevated and she squirmed restlessly against Rowdy, unexpected jealousy rose so quickly it made Dolan sway. He wanted her sexy voice speaking to him—her moving against him like that. Anxiously, he rubbed his palm across his chin, before tugging at the tip of his mustache.

Dammit. More than anything in this world he wanted to hear her cry his name. Beg him to take her again and again.

What the hell was the matter with him? She was only a woman—one who had been a thorn beneath his blanket since she hit town. The realization should have put things into perspective, but as she placed her palms on Rowdy's thighs and glided her hips seductively against his, Dolan's cock swelled, throbbing to a painful beat.

Fuck. Why didn't he just admit it? He was fighting a losing battle. He wanted this woman regardless of the cost.

Stepping forward, he yanked his zipper down and breathed a sigh of relief when his erection sprang forth, easing the pressure. No briefs—he seldom had use of them.

Standing before her, he watched Rowdy's fingertips tease her nipples and make her expression turn dreamy. When her tongue slid between parted lips, Dolan reached out and pulled her to him, knocking away his friend's hands. Heavy eyelids rose, revealing what was undeniably lust. His anger flared. He should have been the one who put the fire in her eyes, the cry in that sexy voice. Well he would rectify that starting now. He pressed his mouth to hers.

As she opened to his advance, his tongue sought hers. They touched, dueled. *Mine*, echoed in his head. He wasn't gentle, his mouth demanding.

To his surprise she let out a growl, sucking his bottom lip between her teeth, and nipped. It was so fuckin' erotic. He slanted his head, deepening the caress and drank from her mouth like a starving man.

The kiss ended and both gasped for air. But he had only begun to pleasure her. Stroking his palm down her throat, his lips followed, tasting the salt of her skin and inhaling the sweet powdery scent of her perfume. Trailing his tongue over the swell of a breast, he bent and sucked the nipple into his mouth. The tip was hard against his tongue, heavenly to his taste buds. Scraping his teeth across the tip, he bit down and she cried out.

Had he been too rough?

She answered his unspoken question by stabbing her fingers through his hair and holding him to her breast. "Yes," she hissed. "Oh God, yes."

He changed breasts to worship the other taut peak, while pinching the moist one hard.

"My turn," Rowdy said, pushing Dolan aside to take over where he left off.

But Dolan wasn't willing to stand back, an observer, while Rowdy turned her on. He needed to mark her—make her his. If he couldn't fuck her pussy then he'd do the next best thing. "I need to taste you."

Still kissing her, Rowdy shifted his body making room for Dolan to kneel between her legs. Inhaling the light pheromones she released made his mouth water with anticipation.

Was she wet? Ready for him?

He ran a finger over the soft folds of her pussy and felt the tremor that shook her. Oh yeah. She was wet. He leaned in and slid his tongue along her slit.

She jerked against him. "Dolan." She gripped his shoulders.

The sound of his name, her touch, sent chills up his spine. "Mmmm... You taste so damn good." He grasped her thighs and widened them. "So moist and swollen."

"Don't tease me." She paused, but only for a second. "Fuck me. Now."

Something inside Dolan snapped. He loved a woman who talked dirty. He buried his face against her sex and growled, stabbing his tongue over and over into her hot core.

"Yes." She made a hissing sound that heated his blood. "Eat me." She thrust her hips, riding his face as she grabbed his head and held on.

Her clit swelled, pressed against his tongue. He couldn't help taking it into his mouth and sucking hard.

Between her soft moans and the wet sounds of his mouth, he barely heard the tearing of paper. That damn Rowdy had moved around to her backside and was preparing to fuck her ass, he just knew it. The thought sent Dolan into a tailspin. He flicked his tongue across her clit once more and then released his hold to push to his feet.

"No." It was a cry of frustration. She grabbed his arm and pulled him to her. "Don't stop." Squirming, she grinded her hips against him as if to assuage the throb he knew pulsed between her thighs. "Fuck me. Do it now." This time she closed the distance between their lips. Her kiss was hungry, demanding and fuckin' hot.

He felt something pressed to his palm and instinctively knew it was a gift from Rowdy—a condom.

His friend shot Dolan a grin, before he placed his mouth to her ear. "Baby, are you ready to be taken by two men? I can't wait to fill this sweet spot with my cock."

Their kiss ended abruptly. Her eyes jerked open, filled with apprehension. "I've never—"

"Shhh..." Dolan brushed her hair back. "We'll be gentle."

Chapter Seven

The breath Tracy held released in a whoosh. Her body was going up in flames. It was difficult to focus on anything other than the ache between her legs. Still Rowdy's words echoed in her head.

Baby, are you ready to be taken by two men? I can't wait to fill this sweet spot with my cock.

Anxiety crawled across her skin as he nudged her ass. She wasn't sure about her next adventure—having two men make love to her at once, but there was something on Dolan's handsome face that helped to ease her mind, some.

He stepped away while she thought of the possibilities. There were only three orifices available for exploring. By the cool, wet substance Rowdy was applying to her ass, she could tell her mouth wasn't one of them. Her butt cheeks clenched together.

Rowdy chuckled, "Relax. You're gonna love it."

The idea of anal sex was frightening and exciting at the same time. Her ex had tabooed the sexual activity, stating it was repulsive. Yet that didn't stop her from wondering and wanting.

While Rowdy stroked her backside in little teasing strokes, Dolan gazed at her with such heat she felt it flicker across her skin like sparks.

Damn. He was sexy standing there in nothing but his jeans. Zipper already down, the material parted revealing dark curly hair and a delicious view of his cock. Slowly, he pushed his pants over narrow hips and down muscular thighs to his ankles.

Oh my. The girth and length of his erection was more than impressive. It was downright sinful.

He kicked his pants away and he took himself in hand stroking from base to tip. She knew his actions were meant to incite and it was working. What could she say? There was something exciting about a man masturbating that sent her senses reeling. Her nipples tightened and streaks of pleasure burned between her legs. As a very naked, very aroused Dolan approached, a wave of desire released. Her heart was beating out of control. She couldn't wait for the moment he filled her.

A finger penetrating her ass made her flinch and cry out in surprise.

Dolan wrapped his arms around her. "Easy, darlin', I've got you. Just breathe. In. Out."

She tried to breathe. Lord, she tried, but the feeling was so strange. The tight opening puckered as if trying to fight the invasion.

Dolan covered his mouth seductively over hers. "Try to relax, sweetheart. Remember to breathe."

How?

He stole the air from her lungs when he pressed his cock between her thighs. In slow thrusts he caressed her swollen folds, rubbing across her clit to send tingles throughout her sex.

"She's so tight." Laughter was gone from Rowdy's voice. "So fuckin' tight," he groaned, before inserting another finger. The discomfort was minimal as he pushed past the ring of muscle.

"She's almost ready."

Oh yeah, she was ready. Coupled between two men, one finger-fucking her ass, the other teasing her slit. Who wouldn't be ready? In fact, she was past ready.

"I need you in me," she admitted to Dolan without shame. "Fuck me." She couldn't wait a moment longer.

A roguish grin tugged at his mouth. "My pleasure." He angled his hips and the head of his cock separated her folds. For a moment, he held her in suspense.

"Dammit," she growled. "Take me now."

Laughter swept over her as he thrust, driving all the way inside. It felt beyond fantastic. It felt—

Tracy's eyes flew open when Rowdy's cock breached her ass. "Ohmygod." The breath she swallowed lodged in her throat.

"Breathe," both men said at the same time. She wet her lips. As she inhaled Rowdy pushed forward.

Yeow!

Her knees buckled. She cried out and Dolan captured the sound with a kiss. The burn was like her ass had been lit on fire. A multitude of sensations washed over her.

Fear.

Pain.

Even pleasure edged the sting.

"You okay, baby?" Concern tightened Rowdy's voice.

Dolan released her lips, looked into her eyes, and then he smiled. "She's good. Right darlin'?"

Unable to speak, she nodded. Quietly they held her, allowing her body to adjust to their presence. Her heartbeat calmed, breathing eased, before they began to move. She braced herself, sucked in a terse breath and held on.

Whatever she had expected to feel didn't materialize. In fact, she was at a loss as to how to describe the exquisite fullness. In unison they thrust in and out of her body.

It was beyond amazing.

The subtle pain seemed to heighten the ecstasy. Higher and higher she soared. Her body and mind lost to what these two men were doing to her. Dolan set the pace, an easy rhythm. Their hands were like those of musicians plucking strings of sensation over her body to make the sweetest music.

Tracy closed her eyes and savored the moment.

Rowdy groaned, his breathing ragged. "Ohhh..." He buried his fingertips into her hips as if he held on by mere threads. When his hard thighs slammed against hers, Dolan picked up the pace. Fast and hard, they pumped in and out carrying her towards the orgasm of a lifetime.

A particularly strong contraction tightened and squeezed her pussy, shaking her to the core. Her eyelids flew open to the predatory gleam in Dolan's eyes. So much hunger—lust. No one had ever looked at her like that.

"Mine," he said with such conviction she could almost believe him.

"I—Oh—" Another contraction stole her words.

"Stay with us," he encouraged. Lord knows she tried but felt her control slip.

Perspiration beaded his forehead. His hand shook as he traced a path between her breasts, down her belly, stopping where their bodies met. "Rowdy?"

"Fuck yeah."

"Now." Dolan reached between them and pressed his fingers to her clit.

She bucked wildly between them. The lights in the room

dimmed or maybe it was her imagination. Like talons tearing at her insides, her climax clawed its way to the surface and exploded.

A scream ripped from her throat. Her body convulsed, shaking uncontrollably. She couldn't breathe—didn't try. Holding on to Dolan she rode the wave, melting into the moment.

At the same time, Rowdy stiffened, pressing against her as tightly as he could. Mumbling something unintelligible, he groaned low.

But it was Dolan's expression of pure rapture as his orgasm approached that enthralled her. He thrust once more, striking the back of her pussy. She felt his cock stiffen and swell. His hips jerked. He threw back his head on a cry of triumph that sent a shudder through her. Desire, agony and finally bliss filtered across his face before he buried his head against her shoulder.

Breathlessly, he murmured, "Mine," and closed his arms around her possessively. The admission slid over her like warm honey.

If only it were true.

Rowdy kissed her neck before he gently withdrew from her ass. She heard him pad across the floor and then the flow of water.

How long Dolan held her she couldn't say. Their bodies were warm and moist pressed together. His steady heartbeat rang in the ear she had lying against his chest. She couldn't see his face.

What was he was thinking? Did he regret the night?

Chills raced across her skin, tightening her nipples. Was her body's reaction due to her thoughts or the blow of cool air that flooded over them when the air conditioning kicked on?

The pipes moaned as she heard the water turn off. His arms dropped from around her. He peeled off his condom and dispose of it in a wastebasket. Returning, he hoisted her up in his arms. She released a small cry of surprise. His arm lay beneath her ass, drawing her attention to the dull ache that existed. Yes. There had been discomfort, but the pleasure far outweighed it. The whole night had been better than any fantasy she had dreamt.

He didn't say a word when she looked up at him. His dark expression was unreadable. The moment was awkward as he carried her to the bed and then carefully laid her down. Placing her heel on his shoulder, he removed the stiletto and let it fall to the floor with a thud. His palms smoothed up her leg until he reached the end of her stocking. With ease he rolled the silk down her thigh, past her knee and off her foot. He held the stocking for a second or two, his gaze hot on her exposed sex. For a brief moment she thought he would go down on her again. Prayed he would. She barely resisted the need to squirm beneath his stare, but he blinked, releasing the stocking, and removed her foot from his shoulder. In was pure hell as he repeated the same process on her other leg. The act was so sensual, moisture built between her thighs. She wanted him to touch her so badly. Take her again. But it wasn't in the cards. Instead he picked her up once more, cradling her in his arms as he carried her toward the bathroom.

Tracy sighed at the sight of the bathroom. Nothing could have been more romantic than the large tub with its pillars trimmed in vines and colorful flowers. The soft hum of the jets blowing and the inviting bubbles called to her. Rowdy lounged in the water. His strong arms rested along the edge. He held up a glass filled with amber liquid. "Join me."

Tracy was prepared for Dolan to set her on her feet. Instead he climbed into the tub with her still in his arms. Carefully he

Mackenzie McKade

sat in the warm water bordering on hot, catching her unaware as he pulled her snugly upon his lap. His semi-hard erection pressed to her ass. The man must have a constitution of an Ever-Ready battery. The thought brought a smile to her lips. If she shifted a little to the right and spread her legs, he would be all hers.

Rowdy handed her his glass. "Baby, you were wonderful."

Heat flared across her face and a burst of uneasy laughter released. "You weren't too bad yourself," she said before raising the glass to her mouth. Even before she took a sip she inhaled the bouquet of toasted wood, earth and cedar.

Ahhh... Whiskey.

It was an acquired taste she had discovered when her ex had gone hunting for the weekend. A bottle of booze and a vibrator had been her entertainment. She tipped the glass and sipped while breathing the scent in to let it linger on her tongue. The best thing about whiskey was that its flavors lasted. Stealing a glance toward Dolan, she couldn't help remembering his first kiss laced with whiskey. It had nearly curled her toes. She offered him the glass, but he refused it.

With a slow sensual draw, he said, "Take another drink, but don't swallow." He must have realized her confusion because he added, "I want to drink from your lips."

Now if that wasn't the sexiest thing anyone had said to her. Her pulse leaped as she turned in his lap. Her hand shook as she tipped the glass. Flavors burst against her tongue, and then Dolan covered her mouth with his.

Damn. The woman tasted good. The whiskey was only a reason to devour her mouth once more. He took his time savoring how soft her lips were. How pliable she was beneath his assault. He left no place untouched, releasing her when he

84

wanted nothing more than to pull her beneath him and have his way with her again. He was about to go in for another kiss when Rowdy grabbed her arm and pulled her off his lap. "I want some of that."

As she began to sink Dolan lunged for her, but Rowdy yanked her safely into his arms. Her sexy laughter was like silk across Dolan's skin as she held her hand high. The whiskey splashed around the confines of the glass, but she didn't spill a drop.

His kind of woman.

In fact, Tracy had been everything he knew she would be and more. She came apart in his arms, leaving him more sated than he had ever felt. Even now his cock was hardening, needing to feel her warmth surrounding it. It didn't help that she looked even more inviting with her skin glistening from the water and her wet hair hanging loose around her shoulders. After tonight he didn't know how he was going to let her go, but he would. They had too much between them to make it work.

His stomach knotted when she straddled Rowdy, sipped from the glass and then leaned into him for a kiss. Dolan swallowed hard, trying to rein in his resentment. Brooding would get him nowhere. Tonight might be the only opportunity he had with his little redheaded veterinarian and he planned to make the most of it.

Water splashed as he crossed the distance between them. A brush of his hand and he wiped the bubbles from her shoulder before he pressed his lips to it. As he caressed a path toward the top of her spine, goose bumps rose across her wet flesh. He felt the tremor that rocked her as he trailed his mouth down her back. "My turn," he whispered against her skin.

She glanced over a shoulder, cocking a brow as she turned the glass upside down. "Sorry. Empty." Her tongue slid seductively between her lips, driving him crazy with need. A groan caught in his throat. No one should be so damn sexy and have a killer voice like hers.

Rowdy wagged his brows. "Problem solved." He reached behind him to pick up the half-full bottle. "Here you go."

Dolan took the whiskey offered him. "Turn around, darlin'."

He began unscrewing the lid as Tracy slid off of Rowdy's lap. She was immediately drawn back down, but this time she faced Dolan. He took a drink from the bottle. The whiskey burned but was smooth going down.

Grinning, she wiggled her ass. "Happy to see me?"

"Baby, you have no idea." Rowdy bucked beneath her, setting off a series of giggles as she tried to stay atop his lap and not slide off, drop the glass, or drown as they set the water to splashing. A large wave rose spraying over the side of the tub. "Dammit." He slowed his pace.

Scrumptious breasts rose and fell as her laughter died and she raised her glass to Dolan. He passed by her extended hand, tipping the bottle so that it ran over one of her nipples and into the water.

Their eyes met and they both began to smile. Flattening his tongue against the hard peak, he licked, savoring both the flavor of the whiskey and woman. He wrapped his tongue around the nub and sucked it deep into his mouth.

She gasped.

"You like that don't you, baby?" Rowdy asked pinching her other nipple between his fingers.

Arching into their touch, she said, "Oh yeah."

The soft expression on her face made Dolan set aside the bottle and reach for her. She went willingly into his arms, her legs locking around his waist. His rock-hard cock nudged her pussy. He couldn't wait to feel her around him again. Angling his hips, he drove inside her. Her mouth parted on a sharp breath.

"Fuck." His jaws clenched from the exquisite warmth. He held her close, grinding her hips against his so that he was seated as deep into her cradle as possible. "So fuckin' hot." He inched his way back to the seat on the other side of the tub and sat. He smoothed his hands down to her ass. "Ride me, darlin'."

Placing her hands on his shoulders, she pushed upward to ease him out of her cove. With more pressure than he anticipated she impaled herself upon him and began a slow rhythm riding him in earnest. The way her body swayed and the sensual caress of the water made his groin tighten. She brushed the hard peaks of her nipples across his chest and he sucked in a breath.

Laughter danced in her eyes. She leaned forward and rubbed against him again. "Feel good, cowboy?" Each word stroked his ears. Damn. Her voice was enough to break a man.

He was just about to show her how good it felt when Rowdy spoke up. "Bring her here."

Dolan glanced over her shoulder. Tracy stopped moving against him and followed his gaze. His friend was sitting on the edge of the tub, legs spread wide, a condom in his hand and a mischievous grin plastered on his face.

Dammit. Dolan had forgotten about a condom. Thank God Rowdy had stopped them when he did. But, fuck, it felt so good.

"Let's see how good she is with her mouth." His friend ripped open the packet he held. "Think you can put this on me—" he paused, "—without using your hands?"

For days Dolan had fantasized about just that. Well, that was he'd dreamt of her mouth wrapped around his cock, not Rowdy's.

"Is that a challenge?" she asked, beginning to rock gently against Dolan. He tightened his grip on her hips.

"Yep." Rowdy took himself in hand and started to stroke from base to tip.

Leaning in to Dolan, she gave him a feather-light kiss. "I'll be back." She hesitated only a second before she crawled from his lap. An instant feeling of loss as he slipped from her body surrounded him.

She drifted through the water toward Rowdy. He handed her the condom and then reclined back, bracing himself on his palms.

Dolan walked around the tub. No way would he miss this.

The condom disappeared between her full lips. Determination flashed in her eyes. She slid between Rowdy's thighs, easing to her knees. Her red hair floated on the surface of the water as she bent forward.

"Here." Rowdy picked up a pair of handcuffs Dolan hadn't seen sitting there. "Secure her hands behind her back."

Tracy's eyes brightened as his friend dangled the manacles before her. Did the thought of being bound excite her?

Dolan took the bindings from him and moved behind her. Carefully he pulled her arms back. The first bracelet snapped around her wrist. She released a muffled cry when the second ring clicked shut. Her chest rose and fell, rapidly.

Damn. She was a pretty sight. There was something about a bound, naked woman, especially this one.

As he walked from behind her, he watched the tip of his friend's dick disappear into her mouth. Dolan's pulse leaped and blood rushed his groin. He could almost feel her warmth around his own erection.

Rowdy raised his hips.

Her brows pulled together. "Hoe thill." Her words were almost unintelligible. It appeared she was having a little difficulty.

Rowdy chuckled, evoking a growl from deep within her throat.

Stubborn. Dolan had pegged her right.

"Use your tongue," he suggested. "Roll it a little at a time."

Her nostrils flared. A little spittle seeped from the corner of her mouth. Rowdy's cock slipped further between her lips. The intensity in her stare as bulges in her cheeks came and went tickled him.

Yet after a short while, she eased Rowdy from her mouth, sat back on her haunches and grinned. He was completely sheathed. "There." An expression of pride appeared on her face.

He cupped the nape of her head pulling her forward. "Baby, you're not finished."

"What? It's d—"

He nudged her lips with his erection. "Take it. I want to feel that beautiful mouth around me."

She swallowed and then leaned forward, taking him inside her. There was something hot about the bob of a woman's head as she gave a man head. The wet sounds of her mouth, her tongue caressing up and down, were unbearable. Add her soft cries of passion and Dolan's cock grew even harder, the ache now bordering on pain.

Rowdy weaved his fingers through her hair. "Damn." He sucked air in through clenched teeth. "She's good."

Fuck. Dolan knew it.

He couldn't stand the moans Rowdy made or the wet ones that slipped from her mouth. It should be his cock in her mouth. He should be holding her. Without another thought, he eased into the water on his knees. Tracy released a muffled cry as his hands folded around her waist and he raised her to move beneath her. Inching her thighs apart, he wasted no time positioning himself at her center. With one thrust he parted her swollen folds and sunk into heaven.

Ahhh... His eyes closed briefly on a sigh of relief. That's what he wanted—needed.

She fit perfectly against him. Her body folded around him so tightly, squeezing and pulling him deeper. She sat back on him and angled her hips in a way that, from out of nowhere, fire exploded in his groin. He tensed, fingers closing around her hips to still her. Holding his breath, he fought to hang on.

Rowdy looked down at Tracy, heat in his gaze as he watched his cock slip in and out of her mouth. "That's it, baby. Take all of me." She must have complied because he groaned, "Shit." The curse a sign Rowdy was as close to fulfillment as Dolan.

Balancing on the edge of his climax, he smoothed his hand over her abdomen and further down until he found the pulse of her desire. Her clit swelled beneath his touch. He pressed down and oscillated his finger, faster and harder. Her inner muscles grew taut around him.

Flames licked down his shaft, but he didn't still his hand. He was determined she would come before he did. Burying his head against her shoulder, he continued to fight a battle he was quickly losing.

Her body convulsed. She cried out around Rowdy's erection. That was all it took for Dolan to release his control, setting his orgasm free. He couldn't move, only feel as a blaze erupted engulfing him. It felt as if he was being torn apart from the inside out, his body enflamed in sensations. The sexy sounds she made as her climax climbed, peaked and then washed over her only intensified the moment.

His senses came back to him when Rowdy rose and began to devoid himself of the limp condom.

Condom?

Well sonofabitch. He'd done it again. Never had he forgotten protection.

What was it about the woman he held pressed against his chest that diminished his control as well as made him throw caution to the wind? They had enough issues between them. Now was not the time to introduce a baby into the mix.

Lord knew he wasn't ready to be a daddy.

Chapter Eight

Towel drying her hair, Tracy couldn't believe she'd just spent the night wrapped in two men's arms, especially those of Dolan Crane—her adversary and competition. The evening had been amazing—he had been amazing. Even now her blood heated with memories of his hands roaming her body. It had been unbelievable.

Folding the towel and setting it on the counter, she reached for her bra sitting next to it. As she clasped the bra and pulled it over her breasts, the silk rasped across her sensitive nipples. She cringed, gasping as bittersweet pain splintered throughout the peaks. When she raised a foot to slip her panties on, the sweetest of aches rose between her thighs.

Mmmm... She dragged the briefs up her legs to rest on her hips. Her body felt deliciously sore, alive. Not only her body, other senses seemed more acute, unusually heightened.

She could hear Dolan's and Rowdy's muffled voices in his master bedroom. Of course, the spicy scent of Rowdy's cologne lingered in the bathroom, but there was something more. A cool breeze from the air conditioning caressed her. She inhaled and a smile crept across her face. It was her skin. She carried both men's scents. She looked at her reflection in the bathroom mirror. Her flesh was still pink from the warm bathwater. Her lips were red and swollen from their kisses.

What lay ahead for them?

The boys had asked her to spend the night, but she didn't want their time together to be diminished by morning-after regrets. Leaving on a high note would make this experience as close to perfect as it could get. Or was she seriously deluding herself to think it would be easier this way?

Her confidence took a nosedive and her grin faded. What happened between them was sex, nothing more. They were adults fulfilling each others' sexual needs. No commitments. No obligations. Accepting the truth would make it easier to walk out of Rowdy's home and not look back.

If that were true, then why did it hurt so much? She pulled on her pants, fastening them as moisture dampened her eyelashes. Blinking several times, she tried to brush away the sadness that stole over her.

Angrily, she pushed her arms through her shirt. "You're being ridiculous." Rowdy and she had parted ways before and she hadn't felt this emptiness. This time was no different, she rationalized, focusing on the buttons of her shirt. Damn. Her fingers felt like they were all thumbs or was it the sudden tremor in her hands?

Truth was Dolan had made this time different.

This time her heart had been engaged. Bottom line, from the first moment she laid eyes on him there had been something about him that intrigued her. Not even the roadblocks thrown in her way had deterred her attraction for him. She wanted this man.

"Well, missy, he's not yours for the having," she chastised. There were more important things than her lustful cravings. She had to think of Sheldon. He was her responsibility now. The thought was scary.

Shelly had been both mother and father to her son. She

had fit into the parenting role with ease, while Tracy had sought education and a career. Helping her nephew with his school work would be a piece of cake, but what about the other stuff? What did she know about the things a little boy needed to grow up to be a good man?

Her eyes grew misty again. Man, she missed her sister. A few tears fell before she could stop them. Grabbing a tissue she dabbed her eyes and blew her nose.

Glancing into the mirror again, she mumbled, "Crap." Traces of sorrow brightened her cheeks and nose. "Great. I look like Rudolph," she grumbled, digging through her purse to find her face powder. A swipe here and there, she got busy masking her emotion.

After slipping her feet into her shoes, she checked her appearance once more, grabbed her purse, and then she opened the door and stepped into the bedroom.

The minute her gaze fell upon Rowdy and Dolan standing next to the big four poster bed her stomach did a double somersault into a full layout. Neither wore shirts, only jeans.

Damn. She'd never forget tonight.

They glanced at her at the same time. Disappointment shined in Rowdy's eyes. Once again Dolan's expression was blank, unreadable. Muscle rippled beneath his golden skin as he tucked his thumbs into his jeans and leaned against a bedpost.

"I see you didn't change your mind," Rowdy said, moving to take her into his arms. He pressed his lips softly to her forehead. Dolan stayed put and for some reason she felt his sting of rejection.

Forcing a half-ass laugh, she said, "Unlike you, some of us have to work."

Rowdy didn't start his new job for another week. She on the

other hand needed to unpack, clean, find a babysitter, and continue to establish her career. Tomorrow she had several appointments and one particularly important one. Before she had arranged to move to California, she had written Dr. Zimmerman regarding renting office space. He had agreed to meet with her, informing her that he was currently sharing the office with another veterinarian. What she hadn't known is that said doctor would be drop-dead gorgeous and irresistible. To complicate matters, she had no doubt this meeting would drive the wedge between her and Dolan even deeper, but she couldn't let that be a factor in her decisions. What happened tonight would need to be forgotten, starting now.

"Maybe you two should take a couple days off. We could go down to Mexico, play in the sand and drink tequila." Rowdy grinned.

"Can't," Dolan answered before she could speak.

"Sorry," she added. "I still haven't unpacked and I have appointments that can't be changed."

"My loss," Rowdy said. "What about tomorrow night? Same time—same place." He looked at Dolan and then her, awaiting an answer.

This time she beat Dolan to the punch. "Can't." She didn't offer further explanation.

"Maybe we can hook up this weekend," Rowdy continued.

"We'll see." But she knew tonight had been the first and the last time the three of them would be together. Sheldon was arriving in less than two weeks. She cleared her throat. "Thanks for a wonderful evening."

Placing a finger beneath her chin, Rowdy raised her gaze to meet his. "No." He smiled. "Thank you." Lowering his head, he pressed his mouth to hers. The kiss was tender. When his caress ended he rubbed his nose against hers. "Man, I wish you were staying tonight."

She smiled up at him. "Me too." And she meant it with all her heart. Releasing a heavy sigh, she stepped out of his arms and was immediately pulled into Dolan's embrace.

Where he came from she had no idea. What she did know was that he was a masterful kisser, teasing and caressing her lips with his tongue before pushing inside. Her purse slipped from her shoulder. She heard something scatter as her bag hit the ground, but she was preoccupied when the caress turned heated. He wasn't gentle, his touch more aggressive, almost punishing.

Tracy's pulse leaped. Her heart sped. She fought for control, but it was futile. He was too strong—too virile—too fuckin' sexy. His kiss left her breathless. Sliding her tongue over tender lips, she tasted him once more.

But evidently he wasn't through with her. "Stay tonight," he whispered in her ear.

Chills raced across her arms. She could have sworn she heard the sound of her resistance cracking, threatening to crumble. "I can't."

"Can't or won't?"

She had to be strong, but it was hard when he looked at her with such intensity. Almost as if he expected her to lie. "Both."

His arms fell from around her. He took a step backward and it felt like he was placing more than distance between them.

She inhaled a shuddering breath and tore her gaze from his. Bending down, she started to gather the things that had slipped from her purse. Slinging her bag over a shoulder, she got to her feet. "I'd better get going."

"I'll get dressed." Rowdy picked up his shirt from the floor and put it on. He strolled into the closet, returning wearing sandals instead of boots. They walked to his truck in silence. As he opened the passenger door, he asked, "So when are you going to tell him?"

"What?" She started to climb in, but he grabbed her arm.

"Dolan?"

"Dolan?" She shrugged out of his grasp and climbed in. Looking down at him she attempted to hide her growing unease. "I don't know what you're talking about."

"Sure you don't." He slammed the door before moving around the vehicle. Opening his door, he slid behind the wheel. "I've never seen two people so hot for each other. You like him. He likes you."

She snapped her head around to face him. "You're crazy." She swallowed the pulse throbbing in her throat. "Besides I don't even know him. I mean past the fact that he hates me because I'm threatening his career." Her voice climbed an octave. "Tonight—was just one of those things. It just happened." She wet her lips and turned her head to look out into the night. "It won't happen again."

He started the engine. "Uh-huh." She didn't miss the skepticism in his tone. In fact, it pissed her off. Preparing to give more reasons why she would never sleep with Dolan Crane again, she waited for Rowdy to say more. Yet he remained silent, shifting the truck into gear and accelerating.

Why Tracy felt it necessary she didn't know, but she added, "I mean it, Rowdy. It won't happen again."

"Trying to convince me or yourself?"

She jerked her head around. "Smartass."

He looked straight ahead, but she saw his grin.

Dolan stood at the window, staring at Rowdy's taillights fading in the distance.

Dammit. He shouldn't have let her go. What the hell was he thinking?

Removing his hold, he let the heavy curtain fall. "It's for the best." Even as he said the words, he knew it was a lie. The chemistry between them was unmistakable, he knew it and he'd lay a bet so did she. That's why she left or was he kidding himself?

He pushed his fingers through his hair. "What the hell am I gonna do?" Now that he'd had a taste of her, he didn't know if he could turn and walk away.

Irony echoed in his laughter. The little redhead veterinarian could ruin his bad boy reputation. Then again, he could lose more than his reputation to her.

Dr. Zimmerman had informed him earlier today he was meeting with Tracy tomorrow. She was inquiring on working out of their office. Doc and Carl Epps were friends. Of course, the old doctor had asked Dolan what he thought about the idea of her joining them.

He had treaded lightly, stating that it could get pretty cramped since the office had been built to accommodate two, not three, veterinarians. There would be additional office personnel expenses, conflicts in the operating room and use of equipment. Zimmerman had brushed away each one of his worries, stating he was doing less and less in the office.

"My hands aren't as steady as they use to be. Besides you're performing the majority of my surgeries. In reality there would still only be two doctors. And I hear she's a looker." Doc had nudged Dolan's arm and winked. "She's intelligent, loves horses and what she does. Hell, boy, she even comes from your ol' alma mater."

His mentor continued to inform him Tracy was a graduate of the Ohio State University College of Veterinary Medicine. Dolan learned she had earned a full scholarship as he had.

"Like you, son, she needs a chance to get herself established."

Damn. Did he have to play that sympathy card?

If it hadn't been for Zimmerman, Dolan didn't know what he would have done after graduation. Of course, he could have gotten an internship with one of the other veterinarians in the city or in a different state. Yet Doc had his foot into some of the most powerful breeders and racers in California. Contacts, networking and opportunities that would have otherwise been elusive were handed to Dolan. Not to mention, he could study with one of the best. But it had been Dolan's knowledge and work ethic that had taken him further.

Of course, there was another way to look at this situation. If she didn't establish herself in California she would leave. Sounded pretty much like a lose-lose situation. Helluva choice. Either they compete for business or she was gone.

Is that what he wanted?

Before he could answer his own question he heard a cell phone ring. This late at night it had to be an emergency. He checked his phone. Not his.

The ringing stopped, but immediately started up again. He cocked his head and listened. The sound seemed to be coming from the overstuffed chair. Bending low, he saw a glint of shiny metal and reached for it.

Tracy's?

He pressed the call button and placed the phone to his ear.

"Tracy?" a masculine voice asked. Immediately Dolan felt

his gut tighten.

"No," Dolan snapped.

"Who is this?" the man on the other end demanded. "Where's Tracy?"

"Dolan Crane." He wasn't giving any information out until the caller identified himself. "Who is this?"

"Crane. Thank God. This is Carl Epps. I'm looking for my niece." There was a moment of silence. "Why the hell do you have her telephone?"

"Didn't know it was hers. Guess she misplaced it." Dolan was used to irate fathers. Now he could add uncles to the list of individuals worried about his soiled reputation.

"Where is she?"

A lie was probably better than the truth that he and Rowdy had just spent several hours wrapped in his niece's arms. "Don't know. Is something wrong?"

"Yes. It's Ice Princess. She hasn't eaten since I picked her up three days ago. First thought she just needed time to adjust. But—not now. She seems lethargic and wandering around in circles. I came out to check on her and she acts like her legs are weak." Frustration and desperation heightened Carl's voice. "Damn the girl. Where is she when I need her?"

"Tell me where she lives. I'll fetch her and we'll head over to your place." Dolan listened as Epps told him she had purchased the old Cartwright homestead. He knew the place well. Trudy Cartwright, the previous owner, was a hoot. "Be there in twenty." He closed the telephone, pocketed it and headed for the door.

Lights shone in the windows of the small ranch home. Dolan smiled. After Trudy's husband passed in the fall, her spirits had dropped. Lonely, she had called Dolan several times on false pretenses, a limp or sneeze from her last remaining horse, nothing that required a veterinarian.

Hell. He didn't mind.

Truth? She was the closest thing to a mother he knew.

As he maneuvered his truck in front of the house, he saw the weathered siding and remembered the paint he purchased sitting on the floor-bed of the truck. Guess he'd have to return it or maybe Tracy—

Nah. What was he thinking?

Still she was lucky. The house was a homey place. Flowers in window boxes and a porch that surrounded the entire structure. A swing gently swayed in the cool breeze. By his recollections, the inside was just as charming.

Wasting no time, he opened his door and exited. His boots sounded hollow against the stairs as he climbed toward the front door. The doorbell was newly installed and so was the screen door, the last things he had completed before Mrs. Cartwright left. He gave the door a couple whacks.

A dog barked. In mere seconds, light flooded the porch. Dressed in an overnight shirt that barely covered her, Tracy stood before him with a gallon of Rocky Road ice cream in one hand, a spoon in the other and an expression of surprise on her face. The smudge of chocolate on her upper lip caught his attention immediately. What he would give to lick away the ice cream and maybe just make her dessert.

He wedged open the screen door. "Midnight snack?" A little ratty-looking dog darted out, yipping as he ran around Dolan's feet. He couldn't stand staring at the dab of ice cream on her lip. Ignoring the ankle biter, he reached out and wiped the chocolate from her mouth with his thumb.

Her tongue followed the path of his finger. "Uh." She

101

blinked and looked down. "Foxy. Get back in here." The terrier-mix was quick in minding. She bounded through the doorway and sat quietly at Tracy's feet. Glancing over his shoulder once more, she asked, "You alone?"

He took the spoon from her hand, dipped it into the ice cream carton, retrieved a big scoop and then stuck it into his mouth. Rich and cold, but he would rather taste the sweetness of her lips. "Yep," he said, licking the spoon.

It took a moment for her to respond as she stared at his mouth. Was she thinking the same thing? Did she want him to kiss her?

The prettiest shade of pink dotted her cheeks when she caught herself staring. Clearing her throat, she straightened her backbone, which raised the hem of her shirt to give him a better look of her long legs. "It's late. Why are you here?"

Dropping the spoon back into the carton, he fished her telephone out of his pocket and held it out to her.

"Crap." She grabbed the telephone. "Thank you. I was wondering where I had left it."

"No problem." He started to step inside, but she move into his path.

There was a moment of uncomfortable silence. Their eyes locked.

"Well good-night."

If she thought she was getting rid of him so easily she'd better think again. "Your uncle called."

"Carl?"

"Something's wrong with one of his horses."

Her eyes softened with concern. "No."

"Get dressed." He extracted the ice cream from her hand. Stepping past her, he headed toward the kitchen. "I'll take care of this and then haul you over there."

"That isn't necessary," she insisted following, the dog hot on her heels.

"It sounded serious. You might want to hurry."

"Serious? What's wrong?"

He raised a brow. "We'll talk about it in the truck."

She frowned, hesitating as if she thought to argue with him, but in the end she turned and hurried off to the bedroom.

Dolan struck his thigh with a palm. "Come on, Foxy. Let's put this away."

The dog yipped, wagging her bushy tail and followed him into the kitchen.

The place looked like a hurricane had hit. Boxes lay strewn about, some open, some not. Crumpled newspaper was thrown around the room. Dishes, pots and pans, and knick-knacks covered the counter and butcher block table.

Trudy would have blown a gasket. She was always so neat and organized. Of course, he didn't know enough about Tracy to start making assumptions. Clearly she hadn't finished unpacking.

Opening the freezer, he chuckled. He set the ice cream down between three other gallons of the frozen dessert. Obviously she had a sweet tooth. He closed the refrigerator and started to unwrap a glass out of one of the boxes on the table. As he grabbed another, she came through the doorway dressed in jeans and a light sweatshirt. She held a black bag in her hand.

Her tennis shoe squealed against the tile floor as she turned. "Let's go."

The look on Uncle Carl's face said he was worried. Fast,

agitated steps carried his stout frame toward the stables as she and Dolan followed. He threw open the barn doors with a little more strength than was necessary, causing them to crash against the sides of the barn. "She hasn't eaten. Seemed listless. Thought she was just anxious about her new surroundings. Now this." He stopped before a corral.

Ice Princess's big brown eyes were dull. She looked confused as she gazed around. Her back legs quivered, too weak to hold her. Tracy opened the gate and stepped inside. The animal didn't stir or acknowledge her existence until she touched the horse's neck. Muscles twitch beneath her palms.

"Hey girl." Tracy stroked the mare feeling the heat of her body. Even before she started to take vitals she knew a fever existed. There was a lot a veterinarian could learn by watching. Ice Princess took an unstable step forward, pressing her head against the wall for support. Her muscles continued to twitch and become weaker.

Dolan stayed outside the corral. He perched a boot on the lower wrung of the fence and carefully observed her.

"Spent a fortune for this animal." Uncle Carl continued to ramble. "Should have known something was amiss the moment she didn't eat. Looks like something is wrong with her nervous systems."

"No," both Dolan and Tracy answered at the same time.

"West Nile encephalitis?" She looked to Dolan for agreement.

He nodded. "That would be my guess." Taking his foot off the fence, he joined Tracy. "There was a recent case in San Diego. Epps, do you have any standing ponds? Places were mosquitoes might breed?"

"Hell no. I take care of my stock. They're all vaccinated. Water troughs and ponds are treated." Color bled from her uncle's face. He looked nothing like Tracy's mother, who was short and petite. At six-foot-three he was a big man. He tore off his hat and ran his fingers through short brown hair. "Shit. The damn mosquitoes nearly ate me up when I picked her up from the seller. What are you going to do for her?"

"The disease is unpredictable in its course, but we need to reduce the inflammation in her brain," Tracy explained.

"She needs to be sedated," Dolan added.

Tracy pushed up her sleeves. It was going to be a long night.

Chapter Nine

Sprawled on a bed of fresh straw, Ice Princess lay on her side. Her breathing was shallow. The occasional involuntary muscle spasm rippled beneath her skin. Feminine hands moved skillfully, hooking up an intravenous line and making sure the sedated horse was comfortable. After ensuring that Tracy didn't need his assistance or any of his employees, Epps had left to seek his bed.

Tracy pulled a wool blanket over the animal, tucking in the loose ends like one would a child. "You'll be just fine, girl," she promised.

Dolan watched her with a new sense of respect. Clearly she cared for her patient, knew what she was doing and didn't need his help. Yet he asked anyway. "Would you like me to start the antibiotics?"

She forced a smile that didn't make it to her eyes. Instead he read concern in them. "Please. Thank you. I should have checked her when Carl brought her home."

He hung the bag of antibiotics on the IV pole, straightened out the line and began to adjust the connection. "Were you aware he had purchased a new horse?"

"Well—" She stroked the mare's neck gently. "No."

"Then you can't beat yourself up over it."

She sighed. "I know." The sadness in her voice revealed it still bothered her.

Conscientious. He liked that about her.

"Did you want me to get you a blanket? A pillow?" If she was anything like him she wouldn't be leaving the horse's side. "It looks to be a long night."

"Thanks, but I'll be okay. You don't have to stay."

He knelt beside her. "I know I don't. I want to."

She cocked a brow. Her backbone stiffened. "Because you don't think I can handle this alone?"

He didn't blame her for becoming defensive. All he'd done since they had met was second guessed her actions. "No. It's obvious you can. I thought perhaps you'd like some company. Besides you might need some of my supplies."

Her expression changed from anger to skepticism. "Don't you have calls tomorrow?"

"Yeah, but I can sleep anywhere."

"I bet." An unladylike snort slipped from her mouth. "Tell me you'd rather sleep on straw in a drafty stable than a soft mattress in a warm house."

"Won't be the first time; doubt it will be the last." He sat down on his hip upon the straw. "So when did you decide you wanted to treat animals?"

She licked her lips drawing his attention. "Small talk?"

He shrugged. What he really wanted was to take her into his arms and kiss that stubborn mouth.

A pause lingered between them before she gave in. "We lived on a farm with all the typical farm animals. I remember doctoring the livestock, even when they didn't need it. Add the fact that I was the type of child who brought home every stray in town. Dog, cat, goat, it didn't matter." She laughed, appearing to finally relax when she eased next to him, her arm brushing his. "I thought my father was going to kill me when I snuck home a baby skunk. Hid Stinky in my bedroom. When Dad discovered him he started yelling and scared the little shit. He sprayed everything, including me." He felt the shudder that shook her. "Ohmygod. It took forever for the smell to disappear." She chuckled, again growing quiet and a little solemn.

He smoothed his hand along her jaw line, lifting her chin with a finger. "You okay?"

"Yes. It's just—" She inhaled deeply. "Dad's been gone for four years. I miss him. He encouraged me to pursue my dream of becoming a vet, and then he never—"

An involuntary spasm forced Ice Princess's leg to shoot out, nearly striking them as he and Tracy scrambled to get out of the way. They rose at the same time, bumping into each other. Losing their balance, they began to fall. He reached, pulling her to him. The sweet scent of straw and woman assailed him as they tumbled together, twisting so that he shielded her from the majority of the impact. Pain splintered in his right shoulder as he struck the ground and rolled to his back, Tracy atop him.

Chest to chest, hips to hips, they lay in each other's arms. He gazed into her eyes. They were like magnets drawing him as he pressed his mouth to hers. He caressed the seam of her lips with his tongue and she opened to him. He swept inside to taste her.

Mmmm... Like honey against his taste buds. He savored her, slanting his head to deepen the kiss. She whimpered, the sound soft and yielding and so fuckin' arousing.

Rotating, he changed their positions until she lay beneath him. It felt so right—where she belonged. Intertwining his fingers with hers, he pulled her arms above her head. She surrendered without a struggle. Wedging his knee between her legs, he pressed into her, needing the clothing barrier between them gone.

Their tongues dueled. The kiss intensified, as well as the pace of his hips rubbing steadily against the V of her thighs. He wanted her—now.

Turning her head, she broke the kiss. Breathlessly, she whispered his name.

"Shhh... Darlin'. Let me make love to you."

"We can't—not here—not now. The mare—"

He stole her objection with another kiss. The horse was resting quietly now. There was nothing they could do unless her condition worsened. It was a waiting game. Why not take advantage of the moment?

Dragging her wrists together, he held on to them with one hand while he smoothed his other hand between their bodies. He held his breath, hoping she wouldn't stop him as he slid his hand down her jeans. He pushed further to feel her curls between his fingers. She inched her thighs wider giving him more access and he smiled. It thrilled him to know she wanted this as much as he did. He slid his fingers across her softness. She was already wet—slick with need. He slipped a digit inside her and she cried out, pulling from his grasp to wrap her arms around him.

Her hips bucked against his hand. "Dolan, please."

"Please what?" He didn't wait for her response. Instead, he pushed another finger deep inside her, working the digit in and out. "You're so wet. Hot," he groaned next to her ear, lovin' the way she thrust, back and forth, into his palm. "God, I want to taste you. Fuck you with my mouth. Taste you as you come."

He felt her tremble, her body gripping and sucking on his fingers as if to draw him farther within. "Stop. You're going to make me—" He squeezed her clit between his fingers. "Oh God." She arched her back, increasing the pace as she rode his hand.

"Woman, you make me crazy." Of course, that was putting it lightly. His cock was rock-hard, his balls pulled close to his body, throbbing like a sonofabitch. He wanted inside her so badly he couldn't stand it. Grinding his teeth, he fought to keep his own orgasm at bay.

Her body pitched and then stiffened. She gasped, pressing her head against the straw as she muffled a cry. A long drawn-out moan resulted. For only a moment she lay motionless. Then her body jerked beneath his moving fingers. He wanted her wild in his arms and that's exactly what he got.

Trying to squirm away from his touch, she mewled, "Dolan. I can't take any more." She squeezed her thighs together, placed her palms against his chest and shoved. But he wasn't ready to release her. "Stop. Oh God. Stop."

Even as she pleaded he felt her pussy tighten. Fucking her hard and fast with his fingers, he knew she was close to another orgasm. Her breathing was labored. Her hips jerked once, twice, until finally her thighs fell apart. Sweet surrender. He could do whatever he wanted—and he wanted to see the ecstasy on her face again as she climaxed.

Tracy couldn't breathe. She was holding on by the skin of her teeth as magical fingers continued to stroke and tease her into a sexual frenzy. One orgasm had not been enough, from the intensity on Dolan's face she could tell he wanted to drive her crazy over and over again.

Maybe it was his touch or maybe the fact that they could get caught at any moment that made every inch of her body come alive. She couldn't believe she wavered on the edge of another climax and so soon. Or that in one night she had sexually experienced more than she had during her entire marriage. She had missed so much. Her tender vaginal tissues stretched to the point of burning, flexed and retracted. A flutter appeared low in her belly followed by a ripple that undulated throughout her pussy.

So close.

Every muscle in her body grew taut. Her release swelled like a wave building and building. As he pushed his fingers deep inside her again, she shuddered around him, exploding with such force the ground felt like it shook. Her head fell back into the straw, her mouth opened as a scream clawed its way to the surface. The sound was quickly stifled with a palm over her mouth.

Caught in the moment, she didn't struggle, only closed her eyes. Groaning low, she was pulled deeper into the delicious flames of sensations licking across her body. Each contraction was followed by a quiver of sensation that filtered through her. Every inch of her burned, until finally the fire died leaving her basking in the afterglow. She released a long sigh.

Damn. That was good. Her heavy eyelids rose to see Dolan's concerned expression.

"Sorry, darlin'." He removed his hand from her mouth and the one from her jeans. "We don't want your uncle or anyone else hearing us." He rolled off her onto his side and pushed into a sitting position before he extended his hand to help her to do likewise. A smile touched his lips as he plucked straw from her hair.

Talk about an embarrassing moment. Like some horny teenager she had just had two mind-blowing orgasms, not only in her uncle's stable but in a bed of straw with a man that didn't even like her. Of course, it didn't help that her body still hummed with desire.

She wanted him again.

More than anything she wanted to strip Dolan naked, feeling muscle and flesh beneath her touch as she ravished him. Her arousal flared when he stood. Behind his jeans he sported an impressive erection. The first step he took toward the sleeping mare almost looked painful. He reached down and carefully adjusted himself.

Tracy pushed to her feet. "Uh. Sorry." Her apology lost something when a chuckle slipped out.

Turning around, he closed the distance between them, taking her into his arms. His expression was unreadable. "You think this is funny?" Her pulse jumped when he grinded his hips against hers.

Damn. He was hard. Just the memory of him buried inside her made her nipples grow taut.

"Sort of," she admitted.

An ebony curl fell across his forehead as he pinned his dark eyes on her. "Paybacks are a bitch, darlin'. I plan on collecting later tonight." His wicked promise made her stomach do flip-flops. He sealed his vow with a demanding kiss that left her head spinning when he finally released her. "Shall we check on Ice Princess?"

Ice Princess?

"Oh yeah." Pulling herself together, she walked toward her medical case, dug inside and extracted a stethoscope. Placing the ear pieces into her ears, she went to the horse and knelt. Firmly, she pressed the instrument to the horse's chest and listened.

"Her breathing appears steady." Tracy could feel Dolan's gaze on her as he spoke. "She seems to be peaceful. The twitches are gone for the moment." He grew quiet. The only sound was his footsteps walking away. Glancing over her shoulder, she saw him reach into his medical bag and extract his stethoscope. "Can I join you?" he asked as he approached.

"Sure." She scooted over as he knelt beside her.

He listened for a moment to the horse's heart, lungs and breathing. "Not too bad." His gaze scrutinized the IVs. "About an hour before it needs to be changed. Have you come across other cases of the West Nile virus before?"

"Actually quite a few." She got to her feet, noticing the straw on her clothes. "How about you?" She was brushing off the last strands of straw when the barn door creaked open.

"Just a couple," he said, turning toward the door.

Uncle Carl entered along with two hands carrying two cots, blankets, pillows and a small ice chest. "Thought you two might need these." One of the men yawned as if he'd been awakened from a deep sleep. As the hands began to set up the bedding outside the corral, her uncle entered the stall and knelt beside the mare. "How's she doing?"

Tracy moved next to him, drifting back down to her knees. "She's quiet. These things take time. We won't know anything for a couple of days."

"Damn shame," he said more to himself than anyone in attendance. "There's drinks and snacks in the ice chest." She didn't miss the cautious way he looked at Dolan and then back at her. "Do you want one of my hands to stay in case you need help?"

Or protection? She almost laughed, thinking it was a little too late. Dolan's bad boy reputation certainly had made its mark in this city.

"No. I think we're good." Dolan spoke up before she could. "Right, Tracy?"

"Uh. Right. We're good."

Or was she?

Control flew out the window when it came to this man. Maybe she needed protection—protection from herself.

"Well—" Carl hesitated as if he was still thinking. "If you're sure." Getting to his feet, he added, "I'll check back in later." He offered her his hand. She grasped ahold and he pulled her up.

Before she let him go, she leaned in and gave him a peck on the cheek. "Thank you."

For a big man it was funny to see color sweep across his face that softened. "For what?"

"For trusting—believing in me." Without a blink of an eye, Uncle Carl had placed responsibility of his stock in her hands. It had been years since they had seen each other. He truly didn't know her or her capabilities, but he trusted her because she was family.

"Just don't misplace that damn telephone again." Before he stepped out of her embrace, he gave her a big bear hug. "If you need me I'm only a holler away."

In moments Tracy and Dolan were alone again. Silence stretched between. Only the shuffling of horse hooves and the occasional snort from the other occupants of the stables was heard.

"Come here." His whiskey-smooth voice slid across her skin sending a shiver through her. Inhaling a terse breath, she pivoted on the ball of her feet to face him.

Their eyes met.

Damn that powerful attraction between them. It sizzled in the air, creating electricity that raised every hair on her arms. No way could things work out between them. She'd be an idiot not to fight the allure. There were too many obstacles lying in their path. Planting her feet firmly beneath her, she didn't move. Nothing good could come from playing with fire.

A knowing smile touched his sensual mouth.

She sighed. His kisses were so heavenly. Tracy gave herself a mental shake. *Focus girl. You're probably just another notch on his belt—a challenge—besides he can ruin everything you're trying to accomplish.*

Dipping his head, he allowed dark lashes to shadow even darker eyes.

Oh yeah. He was dangerous.

He crooked a finger. "Come here." But this time he stepped toward her, setting her heart racing. He continued forward, stopping within arm's length, but he didn't reach for her. Instead he caressed her face with a hot, hungry look of desire.

Momma didn't raise no fool. He wanted her to close the distance between them. Prove to him that she wanted this as much as he did. Well, even if it were true it wasn't going happen. She'd already crossed the line with this man. She had to be stronger.

His hand rose smoothing across her cheek, while his expression grew serious. "I know you feel what's between us."

Thank God. He felt it too. She was beginning to think the uncontrollable pull she felt between them was something her imagination had conjured. Of course, he could just be playing with her emotions.

His gaze stroked her like an invisible hand moving down her throat, sweeping over her breasts to set them to tingle. "The lure's too strong." Every place his stare caressed grew sensitive. His gaze lingered on her hips. When he licked his lips her body went up in flames.

What she'd give to feel his tongue between her legs, moving in and out, teasing her clit, sucking it deep within his hot, moist mouth. The tightening in her breasts increased, followed by one low in her belly dampening her thighs. His gaze stroked back up her body fanning the flames. She was burning up with need.

"No sense in fighting it." He reached for her, but she dodged his grasp. "You want me. I can feel it."

"I have an appointment tomorrow to meet with Dr. Zimmerman." The admission burst from her mouth. "I'm seeking a partnership."

There. She sucked in a breath of relief. If that didn't cool his arousal, she didn't know what would. She could almost hear a door between them start to shut. Before it slammed closed, she felt it suddenly swing wide open when he said, "I know."

Her eyes widened with surprise. "You know?" How could that be? Duh! Of course, Dr. Zimmerman would consult him about bringing another veterinarian on board. What was she thinking? "Then why are you still pursuing me? We'll be colleagues—work side-by-side." Or worse, one of them would be without a job.

"I can't help myself," he admitted. "We'll find a way."

Okay. She didn't expect this, not after the last couple days. He took a step forward and she followed it with a backward one.

The man must be delusional. There was no way this would work out. Still she couldn't help asking. "How?"

He took another step toward her. "I haven't figured that out."

Tracy snorted. Just like a man. Ignore it or put it off and it'll take care of itself. She didn't buy into that theory. "So your suggestion is that we lunge off the cliff not knowing the depth or what's at the bottom?"

This time when he reached for her he caught her by the

arm. "Could be fun."

"Fun?" His touch was warm and strangely comforting. Even still, she spoke her mind. "Could be disastrous."

He pulled her closer so their bodies met. "Maybe—maybe not." Dolan locked his arms around her, as his voice dropped. "Now where were we? Oh yeah—" He covered her mouth with his.

She needed to stop this madness. But the thought disappeared when his tongue slipped between her lips to stroke her own. He sipped at her mouth before sucking her tongue into his, holding it with a strong suction. Before she knew it she was clinging to his neck and returning his fervor.

Dolan was the man she'd been looking for to unlock the passion inside her and ease the ache in her body and soul. He made her feel free, uninhibited.

"I want to taste you," she admitted without shame. Her pulse jumped when lust, hot and wild, flickered in his eyes.

Oh, yes. This was going to be good.

Chapter Ten

The breath in Dolan's lungs froze as the tip of Tracy's tongue darted out to moisten her lips. Did his little redheaded veterinarian just express her desire to go down on him? Take him deep into her mouth?

His cock jerked with the thought of those pouty lips wrapped around him, moving up and down, driving him out of his fuckin' mind. From out of nowhere blood slammed into his loins with unexpected force. The ache almost made him groan aloud, but he held back, not wanting to reveal the effect she had on him.

With desire glistening in her eyes, she gazed up at him and then reached for his buckle. Deft fingers unfastened his belt and the button of his jeans. His zipper made a whisking sound. Her fingernails scraped against the straining head of his cock, causing him to suck in a breath and hold it.

Once again he wore no underwear, his erection pushing past the metal teeth. She smiled upon the discovery. "I like that. Makes me think dirty thoughts at the most naughtiest of moments." Her voice was an aphrodisiac streaming through his veins hot and wild.

"Naughtiest of moments?" he managed to say.

"During a meeting." She ran a fingernail along his cock sending a shiver throughout him. He grabbed her wrist. Light laughter met him. "Maybe standing in front of a crowd thinking of you naked, lying in the hay—"

"Get on your knees," he demanded, releasing her.

Without hesitating, she eased down, staring up at him with anticipation on her pretty face. She reached for the waistband of his jeans, but he stepped away. Her brows furrowed, but she didn't speak. Instead she followed him with her gaze as he strolled toward his medical bag. Reaching inside, he extracted a set of horse hobbles that had doubled as handcuffs on several occasions.

Her eyes widened at the neoprene cuffs with buckle closures and two steel rings connected together by a four-inch strap. A smile graced her lips. "Well, aren't you the creative one. What else do you have in that bag of goodies?"

He reached inside and pulled out a flogger. Would she like the sting of leather on her thighs, her ass? What about her breasts? Damn. The thought of her beneath his whip made him hot. He wasn't into sadomasochism, didn't go into cruelty, but he loved branding a woman with his touch. Skin so pink and sensitive. Her expression when pain mixed with pleasure. His clothes felt too tight, especially his jeans.

Her eyes dilated revealing her interest. Fuck. She just kept getting better and better in his mind. She was made for him.

Laying the throngs across his palm and holding the hobbles, he said, "Behave or I just might have to use this."

"Is that what you want or—" she paused, her chest rising and falling with her increased breathing, "—would you like me to be a naughty girl?"

Holy shit. His cock grew impossibly harder.

He closed the distance between them, moving behind her to drop upon his knees. "Naughty." The whip fell from his hand as he pulled her arms behind her. His hands were shaking as he fastened the hobbles around her wrists. When he was finished he stood to move around and grab her roughly by the back of her head, tangling his fingers in her hair. "I want you naughty, darlin'." He felt his nostrils flared as he gazed down upon her. "I want those pouty lips to kiss my cock before you suck it into your sweet little mouth."

"Oh God," she gasped. Lust burned in her eyes like flickering flames.

Releasing her, he pushed his jeans around his knees. His cock sprung free, eager. He couldn't wait a moment longer to feel her warmth surround him. "Take me into your mouth."

Her gaze was pinned on his face as she leaned in and gently pressed her lips to the crown of his erection.

"Take me, darlin'." He placed his palm on the back of her head, urging her forward. Using her tongue, she stroked a wet path along the edge of his dick. He flinched as shooting rays of heat raced up his shaft. "Don't tease me."

Her laughter was like bells on a breeze. As her tongue swept across his skin once again, he thrust, gliding into her mouth. She gagged on his thickness but didn't pull away. Instead she leaned into him, taking him deeper, her eyes burning with unadulterated hunger. The rapture on her face was the hottest thing he'd ever seen.

Shards of pleasure shot into his balls. "Jesus," he whispered. "Suck me."

Her touch was wet and warm, but nothing compared to when her lips closed around him. The pressure was so intense his knees almost buckled. He choked on the breath he swallowed as her tongue swirled around the crown, again and again.

"Oh yeah." He eased out of her mouth and then back in. Burying his fingers in her hair, he groaned weakly. "Fuck me, darlin'." Every muscle in his body tightened, as he rocked back and forth against her.

The suckling, moist sounds she made were driving him crazy, and then she moaned. The sound vibrated around him causing his entire shaft to pulse. Her eyes darkened, her cheeks hollowed as her head bobbed in long, deliberate strokes. Each one designed to drive him out of his friggin' mind. The glide of her tongue, the way she altered the firmness of her lips was amazing. She didn't take her lustful gaze off him as she fucked him, slow then fast and then slow again. The way she was going he wouldn't last long.

A low rumble emerged from the back of his throat. The ache building in his scrotum was nearly more than he could bear. He captured her head, needing to control, slow the pace. Her teeth skimmed along the prominent vein running underneath the length of his dick and the muscles of his abdomen clenched.

"Yeah, baby. That's it." He forced himself to breath. "Suck it harder."

As she bore down he growled, thrusting against a sharpness that sent his mind whirling. Her teeth were seductive agony. He gingerly eased back to thrust one more time, feeling the back of her throat tickle the slit of his cock. She gagged, whimpering around his fullness, but she didn't pull back. Instead she loosened her jaw and inhaled through her nose, taking him even deeper. It was the hottest thing he'd ever seen or felt.

He held perfectly still, balancing on the edge of fulfillment. "Damn, darlin'." Her eyes were watery but filled with dark lust. He had never had a woman look at him in such a way.

Fuck. What was it about her that made his mind spin with desire?

She started to shift her weight and the movement was almost his downfall.

"Lord, don't move." He sucked in a breath. "I can't promise I won't come right in your mouth."

But it was too little—too late. Her throat muscles squeezed. She swallowed.

Lord have mercy.

For a moment he couldn't breathe. The pressure was so exquisite as she milked the sensitive head of his cock while stroking him with her velvet smooth tongue. He clenched his teeth, fighting the storm raging inside. He didn't want to come— not yet.

But it was already too late.

She swallowed again and the hold he had on his fragile control shattered. His hips flinched. Lights burst behind his eyelids. Caught in a whirlwind of emotions racing through him, he was almost unaware of his fingers fisting her hair. She cried out around him. But he couldn't think, much less react. Instead he held his breath and savored the liquid heat shooting down his shaft and bathing the back of her throat.

She drank from him. The muscular action in her throat was so sensual—so fuckin' hot that he couldn't take his gaze off her. His cock jerked several times, each occurrence sending a tremor throughout him.

Now this was heaven.

There was still a burn in his crotch when he eased out of her mouth. "Darlin', you're amazing."

Looking up at him, she licked her swollen lips. The soft glow of passion in her eyes squeezed his chest.

What the hell was wrong with him? How could she so easily arouse tenderness within him? Things were happening too fast.

The thought disappeared almost as fast as it rose when she smiled.

Damn. She was adorable and sexy. Kneeling before him with her hands bound and all that red hair framing her sated face was a picture he could live with forever.

"You're not too bad yourself," she said with that voice that shook him to the core.

He guessed it was time to admit that he had fallen hard for her even though it had only been four days since they met. He laughed, stealing a glance toward Ice Princess. Thankfully, she slept quietly.

Moving around Tracy, he reached for her wrists and unfastened the hobbles. "Next time I'll use that flogger on your pretty little ass." He picked up the whip he had dropped earlier. "Would you like that?" he asked against her ear.

She looked over her shoulder. "Next time?" Her eyes grew darker with desire and interest. The woman was a sexual delight.

Hell yes. There would be a next time—tonight or morning.

The image of her moaning beneath his touch as he stroked her body with leather made his cock twitch. "I'm not through with you and the night's still young." Looping his hands beneath her arms, he helped her to her feet.

She turned around to face him, moving her wrists up and down as if they were stiff. "What do you mean? The night is gone—it's early morning, Tuesday. In several hours the sun will be rising."

Tossing the whip and hobbles toward his medical bag, he reached for one of her wrists and began to massage it. "Then we still have time." He hadn't had enough of her—he might never have enough.

"Thank you." She sighed. "Mmmm... That feels good. Although I would have never thought to use hobbles as handcuffs." Her expression went from contentment to amusement to contemplation. "Time for what?"

He slid his gaze over her. "Time for me to strip you naked and fuck you."

"Oh no." She shook her head pulling out of his embrace. "We've pressed our luck as it is. Besides I'll tell you what time it is, it's time to change the IV." For the moment she was right. The IV was down to its last drip.

"But I want you again." The proof was in his hardening cock. He brushed his finger across the sensitive skin as he eased himself inside his jeans.

She watched as he tucked in his shirt and zipped his jeans. Laughter danced in her eyes as she stared at his growing bulge. "Looks like a personal problem."

"Personal? Not on your life, darlin'." He fastened the button to his pants and then his belt. "I plan on sharing some problem solving techniques I've learned with you shortly."

She chuckled, pivoting. Approaching his medical case, she gathered the hobbles and flogger and stuffed them into the bag.

"Hiding evidence?" he teased.

"Someone has to keep their head on straight. Oh my." Her voice rose with a hint of feign surprise. "What's this?" She held a tube of KY Jelly. "Boy Scout training? Prepared for any emergency?"

He held up three fingers and saluted. "C'mon darlin'."

Tracy couldn't help bursting into laughter. What a scoundrel. "I'd give you a hand, but you have two and a tube of lubricant. I'd say you have all you need." She turned her back to him, returning the jelly and extracting the IV bags she needed.

As she stood, his warm body pressed against her. His arms snaked around her waist. "You're being cruel." She loved the gravelly texture of his voice.

"I'm being realistic." *Liar.* Her words said one thing, her body another. Leaning into him she rubbed against him. "Now let me get to work."

Regretfully, he released her and stepped aside.

She paused briefly before moving. Immediately she went to work exchanging the IV. Next she took the horse's vitals. Dolan picked up his hat, squaring it on his head. Leaning against a post, he stood back and watched. His gaze followed her every move, not like he was scrutinizing her, but admiringly.

"You have beautiful hands."

"What?" She pulled the stethoscope out of her ears and let it snap around her neck, the end lying between her breasts.

"Beautiful hands. Feminine but confident."

She smiled liking the thought that he saw her as more than a woman, but as a colleague. Tracy stood stretching; a long drawn-out yawn followed.

"Tired?"

"A little." No. Make that a lot. She hadn't slept well since she relocated to California—not since she met Dolan Crane.

Her pulse leaped as he pushed away from the post toward her. Muscles slinked beneath his tight T-shirt. Each step sensual and predatory meant to drive her out of her mind and damned if it wasn't working. She felt hot all over.

He weaved his fingers through her hair, cupping the back of her neck to pull her closer. "Why don't you lie down?" He smoothed his cheek against hers. Her eyelids closed. "I'll stay up with Ice Princess."

She inhaled his masculine scent. Hot. Spicy. "No, she's my responsibility." Her words were breathy as she wrapped her arms around his waist. She nibbled lightly on his earlobe before tracing a path of kisses down his throat.

"Mmmm. Darlin', don't start something you don't intend to finish."

What was she thinking? He was right. Too easily she could get lost in his arms. Their moment of insanity was over. "We should talk."

"Not tonight. Sleep," he insisted.

"But—"

He pressed a finger to her lips. "Let it go for now, Tracy." She heard the finality in his voice. It wouldn't do her any good to press the issue.

Without another word, she exited the corral and took a seat on the bale of straw outside. Again, he was right. They both were tired. Squirming, she tried to find a comfortable position, but every which way she moved she was poked with blades of straw. The fencing behind her was cold and hard against her back. The cot was looking better and better. Not to mention her eyelids were heavy.

Dolan sat beside her. "Come here." He eased her into his arms and against his chest. She snuggled closer, finding both comfort and peace as she laid her head on his shoulder. A contented sigh pushed from her lips.

The neigh of horses jerked Tracy awake. It took her a moment to recall where she was. Her uncle's barn—Ice Princess—Dolan.

Damn. She'd fallen asleep.

The blanket tucked around her as she lay on the cot was soft, the pillow beneath her head even softer. Eyelids heavy, she'd give anything for five more minutes, but the sweet scent of oats and the thump of hay as work-hands tossed feed into the bins shook her further awake.

Had Dolan put her to bed?

Sitting up, she wiped the sleep from her eyes. It seemed everyone was up but her. There was a buzz of activity. Several horses were tethered outside their corrals. While they munched on breakfast several groomers wiped them down.

"Easy, girl." Dolan's deep, sensual voice touched her ears, but he wasn't speaking to her. Ice Princess was the target of his attention as she struggled to stand. Big brown eyes filled with fatigue widened. Legs quivered beneath her. "That's it. Nice and slow."

Tracy threw back the covers, getting to her feet, eager to help, but by the time she made it into the corral the mare was standing.

Dolan patted the horse's neck. "Good girl." His smile was deliberate and sultry as he greeted Tracy. "Good morning."

Wow. He looked wonderful, while she felt like shit. Sauntering up to him, the horse between them, she couldn't help but wonder if she looked as bad as she felt. "Morning. I'm sorry."

"No apologies. I just got up myself."

She glanced at the cot beside hers and saw that it hadn't been disturbed. "Liar." In fact, new IVs had been started and the stethoscope around his neck revealed he'd already taken the mare's vitals.

He flashed another drop-dead smile that made Tracy melt

inside.

"She's looking good." Uncle Carl broke into her concentration as he entered the corral. She hadn't even heard his approach. "So what do you think?" He narrowed his eyes on Tracy.

She felt the blood drain from her face as she turned to face her uncle. Did she really have to admit that she had no idea? That she'd been sleeping on the job? That she'd dropped the ball?

"Not too bad. It was a good night."

Dolan came to her rescue when he added, "Your niece knows her stuff. Ice Princess might even come through this with no aftereffects. What do you say, Tracy, fluids and medicine for the next couple of days?"

"Yes. Definitely. She'll need to be monitored and kept quiet."

Carl's gaze darted from Dolan back to her. "Good. I'll have my stable manager arrange for someone to be with her at all times. I bet you two could use a shower and some sleep."

A shower? Tracy released a sigh that grabbed both men's attention. "Sounds heavenly," she admitted feeling heat race across her cheeks.

"Do you want me to have one of my men take you home?"

"No need. I can take her," Dolan offered quickly.

It was a moment before her uncle said, "Fine. Hey, Campton." A man bending over checking the ankle of one of the horses glanced up when Carl called his name. "Need for you to take care of Ice Princess while my niece is away."

"Sure, boss." He lowered the horse's leg and headed toward them.

"Campton, this here is my niece, Tracy Marx. You already

know Dolan Crane." Her uncle's foreman had been out of town on business until today or she would have met him when she arrived.

Campton shook Dolan's hand before he turned to Tracy. He eyed her warily as he extended her his hand. They shook. "Ms. Marx." As he tried to release her, she locked her fingers around his.

"Dr. Marx," she corrected, before easing her grip.

Cocking a brow, he looked down at their hands. "Of course." He pulled out of her grasp.

Bastard.

She wouldn't let him get to her. She was tired and that didn't bode well in a battle of wits. "Here's what needs to be done in my absence." Tracy outlined exactly what she expected, ignoring the fact he glanced toward Dolan occasionally to see if he concurred. Thankfully he remained silent, his features not revealing his opinion. "Call me if there's any change."

"Ready?" Dolan asked.

"Not yet." She couldn't leave without hearing for herself the horse was doing well.

Dolan picked up her bag and handed it to her. His gaze flickered toward Campton and her uncle who had begun to talk about another horse. "You don't trust me," he whispered for her ears only.

"It's not that."

His eyes widened with skepticism.

"Really," she insisted. "I just need to check—listen to her." After several minutes she had confirmed what Dolan already knew. The horse was doing much better. She packed away her stethoscope and picked up her bag where he had set it. Walking toward her uncle, she said, "I have an appointment the later part of the morning, but I'll be back afterwards."

He nodded.

Dolan took her bag, holding it in the same hand he carried his own. Pressing his free hand to the small of her back, he guided her toward the door.

Stepping outside, she looked askew. "Thank you." He had covered her ass with her uncle when he could have thrown her to the wolves.

"My pleasure," he returned. Their eyes met and both began to smile. "Now. Your place or mine?"

Chapter Eleven

"She's beautiful." Tracy admired the eight-year-old sorrel thoroughbred. Her superior racing lines and long legs were obvious even heavy with foal. In Midnight Blue's hay days she must have been fast. But that wasn't the only thing that had Tracy in awe.

Dr. Zimmerman's facility was amazing.

From the immaculate stables with their own fresh water supply system to the fibre sand walkways from the yard right up to the start of the gallops. He even had an equine spa.

Two to thirty-five degrees Celsius, the cold saltwater hydrotherapy was great in treating and preventing a multitude of limb injuries. She glanced at the self-contained unit that could service three horses per hour.

Hot damn.

She tried to hide her excitement as she stroked the mare's ankle, but it was difficult surrounded by such luxury. Facilities like this at her fingertips. She had died and gone to heaven. Tracy stared up from her squatting position.

"So how are you adjusting?" Grey threaded Dr. Zimmerman's black hair. In his day he must have been a damn good-looking man. Now sixty-something, he walked with a limp supported by a cane. Arthritis had made its tracks across once strong hands.

She stood, brushing off her palms. "California is beautiful."

He frowned. "I didn't ask about California, girl. How are you getting along? I hear you've already met Dr. Crane." His voice was gruff, but his eyes were warm, comforting.

What? How did he know?

Boy howdy had she met Dr. Crane. She knew what made him tremble. That he liked his lovin' a little kinky. That he was the most virile man she had ever met. But she didn't share those facts. Instead, she calmly said, "Yes, I have."

He struck his cane against the corral, spooking the horse and Tracy. She flinched.

"So?" The man was like a bulldog with a bone.

She shifted her feet. "I gathered Dr. Crane isn't pleased with my arrival. However, I think we've gotten past that awkwardness."

Or had they?

Just because they spent one long sultry night and morning together didn't mean their business problems had been resolved. Her presence would definitely impact Dolan. He was set up to take over when Zimmerman retired. Her presence could change all that.

"Good. Now tell me how you feel about manning the facility while Crane handles the field." He waited until she exited the corral and then closed the gate with a bang.

The clang cut straight through her. Damn. She was jumpy. This job meant everything to her, even if holed up in a facility wouldn't have been her first choice. *Baby steps*, she mentally whispered. Patience wasn't one of her virtues. Yet a girl had to do what a girl had to do to develop her career.

"It sounds exciting," she lied.

He cocked his head knowingly. "Something tells me that

wouldn't have been your first choice."

Shit. The man was intuitive.

"Dad, give her a break." A deep male voice chastised.

Dad? Tracy glanced over her shoulder.

The resemblance was uncanny. If this is what Dr. Zimmerman looked like as a young man, then she had hit the nail on the head. His son was the effigy of strength and power dressed in a pinstripe blue suit and starch white shirt. No boots. No jeans. No cowboy. This man was executive material. Even his smile looked expensive. His movements held a confident air as he closed the distance between them and extended her his hand.

"Zachery Zimmerman."

"Tracy Marx."

He didn't release her hand. "It's a pleasure."

"The pleasure is mine," she said politely.

Truth was she'd never seen a man so—pretty. That's the only word she could find. Black hair and long black eyelashes any woman would die for swept over high cheekbones. Sky blue eyes a woman could drown in. Every feature sculptured, every muscle toned, not from hard work but hours in a gym. Even his fingernails and hands looked like he had a recent manicure and his cologne was a clean, unobtrusive woodsy scent.

The clearing of one's throat broke the trance Zimmerman's son had weaved around her. "Am I missing something?" She could hear an edge to Dolan's voice.

Tracy jerked her hand back.

"Just introductions," Dr. Zimmerman explained.

"Zach," Dolan spoke his name like a curse.

"Dolan," the man returned with just as much animosity.

She looked between them, witnessing their demeanors change, stiffen. There was a story here. Yet she got the feeling it was one better left alone. Sometimes being uninformed was a good place to be.

"Dolan, would you show Dr. Marx around while Zach and I complete our business?" He didn't wait for an answer; he just limped away toward his office.

"Dr. Marx, would you like to join me for lunch?" Zach asked.

The heat on Dolan's face was hard to miss. He looked angry. About the man's presence or the fact he had just asked her out on a date, which was a ridiculous thought. Of course it had to do with the man's presence. Still it was better to keep their relationship on a professional basis. She'd already crossed the line with Dolan.

"Thank you, but I have another appointment after this one."

His smile was breathtaking. "You do have to eat."

"Yes, but—"

"She said, 'no'," Dolan said abruptly.

Zach's smile faded. He narrowed his eyes on Dolan. There was a moment of uncomfortable silence, and then a gleam sparked. "So that's how it is." He turned his attention back to Tracy with that priceless smile now a smirk. His gaze stroked her body with renewed interest.

Something crawled beneath her skin. She wasn't sure she liked this man.

"Zach!" Dr. Zimmerman yelled, holding the door open.

"I'm coming," Zach threw over his shoulder. "Does he know?"

Dolan seemed to mask his control beneath an apathetic

134

expression, but she wasn't so lucky. Tracy couldn't breathe. Every tendon had decided to lock up. Was the heat between her and Dolan so obvious or was this man like his father—intuitive? Did that mean Dr. Zimmerman already knew that something intimate existed between them?

Crap. Crap. Crap.

Somehow she managed to say, "Excuse me?" at the same time Dolan said, "I believe you owe Dr. Marx an apology."

Zach glanced from Dolan back to her. "Of course, my apologies." His expression shifted so easily from sonofabitch to gentleman, she wondered if she had misread his comment. "Dinner? Say you will join me for dinner tonight."

What the—

Not no, but hell no. She wasn't interested.

"Zach—"

"Thank you," she interrupted Dolan. "As I said, I have plans. It was a pleasure meeting you, Mr. Zimmerman." She didn't even offer her hand. Instead she turned her back on him. "How many stables are on the premises?"

"Twelve."

She placed her palm on Dolan's arm and felt the tremor that snaked through him. "I'm eager to see more. Thank you."

"We have additional paddocks for turnout of long-term patients and day boarders." Dolan escorted her down the hall. "We provide twenty-four-hour intensive care for all critical cases with the full utilization of specialized equipment. We could bring Ice Princess here if you wish."

"Thank you, but I've checked on her earlier. I think she'll be okay. Campton seems to be very competent."

Dolan agreed that Campton was competent.

Zachery Zimmerman, on the other hand, was one man he couldn't stand. Bad blood had existed between them since they were children. Their relationship had gone from bad to non-existent when Doc Zimmerman had taken an interest in Dolan. Guess the elderly man hadn't expected his son to seek all the get-rich schemes versus hard work. Although he had to admit Zach must be doing well if the designer suit and black Mercedes were really his.

Possessively, Dolan placed his palm at the small of Tracy's back. Damn. He loved touching her. She felt so right—so his.

The thought of Zach even near her made his stomach knot. Of course, that was ludicrous. He had no ties to her other than his body recognized hers as his other half. That in itself was asinine.

He guided her throughout the building filled with the scents of antiseptic, medicines and of course a variety of animals. They not only treated horses in this facility, but cattle, sheep and the occasional dog or cat.

"I think you'll be impressed not only with our equipment but our staff. Our technicians are some of the best in California." Pride filled his chest. In the last year they had increased their clinical business two-fold. The real truth was that they needed another veterinarian. There was plenty of work. The loss of the colt the other day and this loneliness he was experiencing had him off kilter—not thinking right.

They entered a large room where one female technician held the reins of a large bay gelding while another adjusted an overhead mounted X-ray machine. Dolan and Tracy pulled to a stop, watching. "We have the capability of producing high quality radiographs of most portions of a horse's anatomy. Our consulting radiologists interpret and report on all radiographic studies, providing us the highest quality diagnoses."

The sparkle in Tracy's eyes said she was impressed. He remembered that hungry look staring back from a mirror once. She'd be perfect here.

"Two portable X-ray machines are available for limited field studies," he added before including, "Beth and Courtney are both certified in radiology and ultrasonography."

Tracy's eyes widened. "You have an ultrasound?"

"Endoscope too," he said. "Ladies, I'd like to introduce you to Dr. Marx. She's contemplating joining our practice." Surprise flittered across their faces, but they smiled and greeted her warmly. Little more was said as the horse stomped its restless legs, demanding their attention.

The thump of Doc Zimmerman's cane on the floor introduced his arrival. He held a manila envelope tucked between his arm and body as he limped closer. Dolan couldn't help wondering what scheme Zach was attempting to talk his father into.

"So do you like what you see?" the elderly man asked.

A tight grin brightened her cheeks a rosy pink. "Yes." She bit her lip and Dolan could see her attempting to curb her excitement. "I'm impressed beyond words."

Doc Zimmerman turned to him. The man's damn scrutiny always made Dolan squirm a little as he mentally gauged him. His silence was deliberate, seeking. "Boy, what do you say we give her a home?"

Not a chance or an opportunity, but a home. Doc was a family man. Even though his son had turned out a loser to the nth degree, he loved him. Now he was opening his arms to Tracy. But the wise old codger had placed the final decision right in Dolan's lap.

Thanks, Doc.

She turned to face him. Her face lost all emotion. She licked her lips and swallowed hard. Beth and Courtney stopped what they were doing; even the horse seemed to be eavesdropping. A pin could drop and it would be the only sound in the room.

The hopefulness in Tracy's eyes made him want to take her into his arms. "I think that would be a great idea." He heard the taut breath she released as relief swam across her face and Doc's as well.

She beamed with happiness, taking a step forward, but pulling quickly to a halt. "Thank you." Extending her hand to him, she said, "I can't tell you how much this means to me."

She didn't have to—he knew. He squeezed her hand before letting her go.

"Good." Doc pushed the manila envelope he held into the hand she offered him. "Take a look at the agreement. If there is anything that gives you heartburn we can discuss it. Now, if you young folk will excuse me, my knee is giving me hell."

Dolan shook his head. He should have known Zimmerman had made up his mind. He was a shrewd businessman, but compassionate. Like Dolan, he loved working with animals— helping those that couldn't help themselves.

"Let me show you the external facilities." He used the excuse to get her alone. As they walked outside, he pulled short. A gentle breeze teased her hair. "Let me take you to lunch."

"I can't. I already have plans."

A wave of disappointment assailed him. He had thought her excuse was fabricated to decline Zach's invitation. A spark of anger flickered in his gut. Had she been attracted to the weasel?

"Rowdy's coming over at noon to install a ceiling fan. I

promised him lunch." She licked her lips again, a nervous trait he was beginning to love.

He resisted the urge to take her into his embrace—to kiss her.

She looked up through thick lashes. "Um." Her voice softened. "Would you like to join us?"

The heat that zinged between them was unmistakable. His cock stirred restlessly behind his zipper. He exhaled. Working beside her night and day would be a slice of heaven and hell. If that beautiful body didn't do him in, the husky sound of her voice stroking over him would. Unconsciously, he leaned closer and reached for her, but she stepped from his grasp. Concern filled her eyes as her gaze darted around. That's when he saw Kerry exercising a sorrel in a nearby arena.

The tech nodded, his hands full. He held a whip in one while the other controlled the long longe line connected to the filly's halter as the horse circled around him. He snapped the bullwhip into the air and Dawn's Break broke into a gallop.

Dolan watched the two-year-old's stride and the bound front ankle. He nodded with satisfaction. "She's doing well. Looks like it's almost healed."

"Yep," Kerry said cracking the whip once more.

"Noon?" Dolan's tone lowered as he directed his attention back to Tracy. Before she could answer, he said, "I'll be there."

"Okay." She released the air from her lungs and then quickly inhaled another sharp breath. "I guess I'd better get going. Uh." She paused. "Thank you." Her eyes were filled with unashamed gratitude.

So innocent.

So sweet.

Yet the moment felt a little awkward. Her fingers flexed as if she thought to shake his hand. Instead, the cutest little grin curled her lips. "Thank you," she repeated before walking away.

He watched her leave, unable to tame the smile on his face. She did that to him, made him giddy with just a smile. A whistle found its way to his lips as he headed back inside to check his schedule. No matter what, he was clearing his calendar for lunch and maybe even a little dessert afterwards.

Chapter Twelve

Tracy couldn't remember the last time her kitchen looked so good and it had nothing to do with neatly aligned pictures. Nor could her feelings be attributed to the squeaky clean wood floor or polished stainless steel sinks she had worked on earlier this morning before heading to Dr. Zimmerman's office. Nope. The credit went to the sight of two ruggedly handsome men standing on ladders.

Dolan and Rowdy both had frustration written across their lowered brows. Parts missing and a mishap with the wire strippers had turned their little task into a battle of wills. Neither one of them would quit until the fan was rotating above them.

No problem. She'd just stand next to the table, slicing cantaloupe into bite sizes, watching their every move. The fruity scent filled her nose, but it was muscles flexing beneath T-shirts stretched over broad chests and biceps bulging that made her sigh and drag her gaze downward. They both had gorgeous asses wrapped in blue denim.

Desire fluttered low in her belly.

What would they do if she unzipped their jeans and peeled them down their legs?

A chill raced up her back, causing her to shiver. Her breasts ached beneath the spaghetti-strap sundress she chose to wear, along with a just a thong. Cool air stroked her legs, making her aware of how easy it would be to slip her panties off.

It was true what they said about lingerie, or lack of, making a woman feel sexy. She was so entranced in her thoughts she didn't notice the knife until it sliced the tip of her finger.

Yanking back her hand, she released the blade to clink against the table she stood before. "Shit." She pushed the injured digit into her mouth. Sucked, tasting the bitter, metallic flavor of blood and the juice of the fruit she had once held.

"You okay?" came a deep, dark voice from above her. She jerked her head up as Dolan released his hold on the fan.

"Ugh," Rowdy moaned, bearing the weight. "Thanks, buddy." He heaved the fan into the bracket anchored to the ceiling, while Dolan shimmied down the ladder.

The legs of a kitchen chair scraped across the floor as he pulled it out from beneath the table. "Sit down. Let me see what you've done." She eased her finger out of her mouth and held her hand out to him.

Gone was the shock and sting of the cut. Instead she wondered if he knew how lethal his eyes were.

Dark.

Mysterious.

So damn sexy she felt her breath catch when his fingers tightened around her wrist. A blistering wave of desire quivered through her limbs. Taut nipples rasped against her dress, awakening a tingle that splintered through her breasts.

"Do you have a first aid kit?" he asked.

"First aid?" she repeated as he dabbed her finger with a nearby paper towel. "Uh. It's just a little cut," she insisted even as she basked in his attention.

What would it be like to have a man worry about her? Someone who would seek out ways to keep her safe, happy and content?

She pointed to the drawer she had designated as the junk drawer. "I think there's a Band-Aid in that top drawer."

He released her and headed for the drawer, providing her with another look of his ass. "What about an antiseptic?"

She stood needing to ease the ache that throbbed between her thighs. "Don't know if I've unpacked it. A Band-Aid would do just fine." A cool breeze caressed her bare skin. "Really. I'm okay." She glanced to the ceiling and smiled as the blades of the fan spun.

Rowdy slipped behind her startling her as he pressed his body to her back. "Mmmm... You look and smell good enough to eat." He pushed a strap to her dress down and pressed his lips to her shoulder. "Yep. Edible." His kisses tickled causing her to chuckle.

"Stop that." She tried to shrug away, but he folded his arms around her waist pulling her close.

He spun her around in his arms. "What do you say, Dolan?" A soft, nervous squeak slipped past her lips when he picked her up and placed her on the table, the surface cold against her bare ass. "Ready to eat?" The smokiness in his voice told her he didn't mean the fruit salad she had planned.

His palm skimmed her shoulder taking with it the other strap, but he didn't stop there. Nudging the bodice of her dress down, he revealed the swells of her breasts but stopped short of divulging her nipples. "Oh, baby." He stroked her exposed skin with a heated stare, making the tips pucker. It didn't help when he raised his hand, fingers plucking playfully at the sensitive peaks.

"Rowdy," she breathed.

He didn't expect to take her on the kitchen table? Wasn't that just a fantasy, one involving things like tongs, basters, and *ohmygod—ice cubes*. She gasped as her knees were pried apart. Her leg bumped against his hard-muscled thigh before he slipped between them.

Spearing his fingers through her hair, he brought his nose to hers. Lust simmered in his eyes. "Would you like to be Dolan's and my lunch?" He inched closer, the bulge between his legs pressed against her thong-covered pussy—a really damp pussy rippling with need.

Tracy didn't trust her own voice at that moment. Her pulse was racing. The tautness in her chest grew tighter. A brief second of sanity peeked through her hazy mind. Her gaze slid sideways seeking Dolan. He stood by the sink, a single Band-Aid in his hand. His eyes were dark. His chest rose and fell. Silently he watched them.

Rowdy pressed seductively against her, rocking so that his stiff jeans pressed against the V of her thighs. She raised her eyes to meet his. "Well, baby?"

"Can't?" she squeezed the word through thin lips. But his caress felt so good. She couldn't help easing against him. "Shouldn't."

"But you will, because it's what you want." His warm palm slid up her arm. "You want both of us buried in that sweet pussy and ass—fucking you hard and fast."

The picture he painted made her heart skip a beat because that's exactly what she wanted. Soft booted steps drew her gaze toward Dolan. Her pulse leaped. There was something about this man that made her reservations non-existent. Each step closer was like gas to a flame, driving her desire higher and higher.

Strong hands reached for her shoulders, drawing them

down on the table. Dolan's hot gaze followed the lines of her legs as Rowdy raised the hemline of her dress, inching it up so the fragile fabric of her thong was the only thing that stood between them.

He smoothed his palm down her belly, stopping at the elastic of her panties. A single finger traced the edges. "Do you want the pleasure?"

Dolan's jaw was clenched. The tendon in his neck defined. He didn't say a thing. Instead, he brushed his friend aside and moving between her thighs.

His nostrils flared. No foreplay or teasing, instead he coiled his fingers in the crotch of her thong and gave a vicious tug. The ripping sound made her arch and incomprehensible words spilled from her lips. She had never experienced anything so primitive, so friggin' hot. Spasms shot through her core, forcing a groan from her throat. Her body became a furnace, heat waves surging across her skin.

"Such a beautiful pussy." His wicked fingers smoothed across the sensitive surface of her folds.

"Oh God." She raised her hips aching for more.

He held her gaze in an intoxicating web of arousal as he stroked her, once again eliciting the same response. "You like that, darlin'?" His tongue slid seductively between his lips.

Tracy was lost.

"Yes," she whispered. Unbelievable. Not only was she giving in to her desire for this man, but excited to be touched by Rowdy too. "Please." She even begged for it.

"Please what?" he teased, nudging a knuckle across her clit.

A shudder raced up her spine. "Fuck me."

When he pushed a finger between her slit she sighed, but

the fullness was short lived. He dragged his hands to her thighs. Without a word, he smoothed his palms along her legs, easing her dress up to expose her abdomen. Holding her gaze with his, he leaned forward and pressed his lips lightly to her belly button.

Damn. He was good looking. Hunger and need reflected in his eyes setting her blood to simmer. She wanted him—craved his touch.

He inched the dress higher, baring her breasts. A whisper of air swirled around her areoles to pimple the skin. "Beautiful." Knotting his hands in the material, he dragged the garment higher until it blocked her vision and trapped her arms above her head.

Her senses went on overload. She could hear his heavy breathing and that of Rowdy's as he stood watching them. The fan made wispy sounds above her. The table was cool. Dolan's hands were warm. She inhaled and even through the cloth she could smell the musky scent of cologne and male desire.

Tracy startled when his fingers caressed her again, thumbs stroking down her slick slit from top to back. "Damn, darlin', you're wet."

Her response was to anoint him with more of her juices as butterfly wings beat against the walls of her abdomen. The flutter increased when she felt his breath and the tickle of his moustache against her thighs. In fact, every muscle from her head to her toes clenched with dizzy expectation.

"Let's rid you of this." Rowdy pulled the dress over her head, letting it slip through his fingers to land on the floor.

She pulled in a shaky breath, blinking to adjust her eyesight. Lord. There wasn't anything as sensual as Dolan's dark head between her thighs. He winked, lowered his head, and her heart skipped a beat. Flattening his tongue, he caressed her slit, causing her pulse to leap again. With long, slow licks he circled her clit.

The clink of glasses pulled her attention to Rowdy as he began to clear the table, transferring the dishes and food to the counter. He removed everything except for the salad bowl. With mischief in his eyes, he took his time in selecting a juicy red strawberry from the bowl. Gently he began to rub the sticky substance around each of her nipples. The swirling air above caressed her nubs into even tighter peaks, and then he leaned in, taking one into his mouth.

Warm. Wet.

Electricity shot through the peak.

Was it the idea of two men cherishing her body or the fact that Dolan took that moment to latch onto her clit and suck in earnest that made her gasp?

"Oh God." A shockwave tore her back off the table. She stabbed her fingers through Rowdy's hair, raising his head from her breast. He flashed a knowing grin of satisfaction. Clearly he knew they were driving her crazy.

The throb between her thighs pounded relentlessly. She needed them now. "Please." She was back to begging. Her hips jerked, pushing into Dolan's caress. "Now." She squirmed. "Need you now."

"Yes, ma'am," Rowdy said with a southern drawl that was so not him, but sexy as hell. "What do you say, partner? Shall we give her a ride?"

"Fuck yeah." Dolan's hot gaze trailed up her length. He stood and grasped her ankles, setting her feet on the table, knees apart. Then he reached for her hand placing it where his mouth had been. "Keep the fire burning, darlin'. Touch yourself." Then he stepped away.

A single finger circled the moist bud between her thighs. Blood surged into Dolan's groin. The bittersweet pain welcomed. Her touch was tentative. A blush tinted her cheeks. Had she ever masturbated in front of a lover—make that two? The innocence on her face revealed she hadn't.

"Don't be shy, baby," Rowdy coaxed, recognizing the same. "There isn't anything hotter than a woman pleasuring herself."

Dolan had to agree with his friend, especially watching this woman seek her fulfilment. Heavy eyelids were shuttered. Her movements were timid; her legs trembled, matching the tremor in his own hands as he unfastened his belt buckle and jeans. His cock sprung from its confines, hard and ready.

Pulling his shirt over his head, he toed off one boot and then the other, unable to turn his head from the erotic sight. She looked at him with heat and fire burning in her eyes. Her touch more confident as her fingers disappeared inside her sweet core, pumping in and out. He couldn't wait to get her alone. Teach her to enjoy performing for him.

"Pinch your titty," Rowdy growled. His shirt was off. He did a couple hops, pulling at his boots.

Her fingers plucked at a nipple as her mouth parted on a gasp.

Damn. This was killing Dolan. He had wanted to move slow, watch as she pushed those delicate fingers in and out of her pussy, but he needed to feel her body surrounding him.

Dragging his jeans down his legs, he stepped out of them. "You're so friggin' hot." He pulled a condom from his pants and let them fall to the floor as he began to tear open the package.

She whimpered a soft sound that went straight through him. Taking his cock in hand, he stroked several times before rolling the sheath over it. Her eyes grew dark, intense. Another step and Rowdy stood beside him.

"I think she likes watching us as much as we do her," Rowdy chuckled.

Come glistened beneath the latex as Dolan ran his palm up and down his dick once again.

"Oh," she cried. Her back bowed off the table. It was the most arousing picture he had ever seen, naked and lying on a table fucking herself. Her hair haloed her head like fire.

"Resist it, darlin'." He wanted to feel her inner muscles seize him, shaking and quivering, as she came apart in his arms. Her breathing was shallow and quick. She trembled. She was almost there—almost ready.

"Your lead," Rowdy muttered. "But make it quick." His voice held an edge of urgency, one that Dolan knew all too well as he walked between her legs.

"Dolan?" She spoke his name as a plea.

Damn. Tracy made him yearn for right now and what it might lead to in the future. She was the type of woman he could see himself working beside and, yes, settling down with.

Reaching for him, she pulled into a sitting position. "I can't wait any longer." Her palms were warm on his arms, her body cool against his chest as she pulled him nearer. He pressed against her cradle. She was wet, hot with need.

"Soon," he promised lifting her into his arms.

"Now," she insisted.

Amusement curved Rowdy's lips. "Impatient, isn't she?" He chuckled, heading toward the living room.

As Dolan followed, carrying her, she corrected, "Horny." Her lips were soft, nuzzling against his neck. Standing in the middle of the living room, he let her slid down his body.

"Head or heel?" Rowdy said with heated excitement.

Confusion furrowed her brows. "Head or heel?"

Dolan didn't want to share her. He wanted her all to himself, but it was too late to say anything now. Besides he wasn't sure about her feelings for him. Would his possessiveness turn her away?

He couldn't let that happen.

"On your hands and knees," he growled between clenched teeth. "I'm heeling." Tracy was his. If he had his way no man would ever fuck her pussy again.

Without hesitating, she drifted to her knees, gazing up with weighted eyelids. Something inside his chest clenched. He wasted no time kneeling behind her.

Dolan smoothed a palm down her back and then held on to her hips. "Such a pretty ass." He'd fuck it one day, but not today. He wouldn't take her without being properly prepared for his entry and now wasn't the time to ask if she had any lubricant.

Rowdy knelt before her. "Open up, baby. I want to feel that beautiful mouth around my dick."

A growl rumbled in Dolan's throat as red-hot jealousy rose. This would be the last time he'd share Tracy with another man, including Rowdy. As her lips closed around him, he grinned from ear to ear.

Damn. This was going to be hell.

Dolan thrust his hips a little aggressively. Not only did he bury his rock-hard cock deep inside Tracy, he caused her to groan and then gag as Rowdy pressed deeper.

"God damn," his friend cried out. "You're not going to believe how good this feels." He rocked to the rhythm of her head bobbing. His features bathed in ecstasy.

The hell Dolan didn't know how talented she was. He eased out of her warmth, attempting to hold on to his anger as he thrust. It didn't help that she made little sucking noises as she feasted on his friend's dick. His hold tightened as he grinded his hips into her, making sure she understood who held her— fucked her.

She moaned. The rapture in Rowdy's eyes revealed he enjoyed the vibration of her throat. He stroked her hair, gave her a look of male satisfaction that made Dolan's blood run cold.

Fuck this. He couldn't remain quiet. The primitive urge to stake his claim overtook him. "Mine," he growled, throwing caution to the wind. Tracy was his woman.

Rowdy glanced at him. The damn man opened his mouth as if to contradict him. Instead a deep-throated groan emerged. His body went perfectly still. His facial features taut.

At that exact moment a fiery burn surged through Dolan's shaft. He eased back trying to control it, but when he thrust again her inner muscles seized, pulling him even deeper.

Oh God. Yes.

He reared back and shot forward one more time, his balls slapping her ass. That's all it took for the floodgates to open. Fire and ice sliced through his veins. Rippling currents overtook his body. They tore through him without mercy.

Someone screamed.

Who? He didn't know or care.

Dolan couldn't think past the exquisite pounding in his groin. In a heartbeat another throb shot towards each of his limbs. Painful, but the best fuckin' thing he had ever felt. He trembled. It hurt so good. His cock jerked with each delicious contraction of her sex, sucking, milking him dry.

Before he knew it, it was over. Yet the thud of his heart against the walls of his chest remained. He felt drained, exhausted, but pleasantly sated. Even Rowdy appeared lost for words as he eased out of her mouth.

Tracy leaned forward, slipping out of his grasp to slide upon her side. Her chest rose and fell rapidly. She didn't make a sound.

"You okay?" he asked.

Rolling upon her back, she stretched like cat, moving her arms high above her head and then down to her side. Through feathered eyelashes she looked up and hummed, "Mmmm... Take me again."

Chapter Thirteen

"So you're the one giving Dolan hell," said the brunette with sky-blue eyes and a friendly smile. She was beautiful. Tall, slender, curves and mounds molded into a pair of jeans, and form-fitting T-shirt that plunged low enough to drive a man's imagination wild.

Tracy hated her immediately.

Well. Not really, but she couldn't help feel a little uncomfortable with the expressions the woman and Dolan shared. She couldn't put her finger on it, but he looked at her lovingly and it didn't feel like a cousinly love.

"Caitlyn." Cord Daily, her husband, tugged on her dark brown ponytail, but it wasn't a scolding, not with the soft way he looked at her. He loved her and it was obvious as his hands drew her back against him, his arms snaking around her waist to hold her tight. Cord tickled her neck with his close-cropped, blond moustache and goatee, causing her to giggle. The sound should have been a high-pitch cackle. Instead it came out a stroke of sensuality. "Behave," he whispered, seemingly unashamed to kiss her in front of God and everyone.

What was Tracy thinking accepting Dolan's invitation to have dinner with his cousin and his wife?

It was Friday. Two days had passed since she'd been with Rowdy and Dolan. She hadn't heard from either of them and

153

probably wouldn't have except today had been her first day at work. It had been a wonderful day working beside Dolan. Caught up in stolen glances and touches she doubted were unintentional. When he had cornered her in the supply room and kissed her silly she had given in and accepted the opportunity to be with him. It was a plus that the staff was great, the work fulfilling. Even Ice Princess was doing well.

Yet since they had arrived at his cousin's, Dolan had grown quiet and reserved. Why?

The mischievous expression on Caitlyn's face said she wasn't through causing trouble. "So, Dolan, she is your type and you like red hair after all."

"Cait!" Both men chimed at the same time. Cord gave her a little shake.

Tracy glanced at Dolan, but he refused to make eye contact.

Coward.

"Okay. Okay." The woman's laughter was contagious. Even Tracy felt a tickle in her throat as Caitlyn danced out of her husband's arms and he grabbed at her, catching air.

So Dolan had mentioned her to them. What exactly did the woman mean by "giving Dolan hell"?

"Why don't you two go do," Caitlyn brushed her hands through the air, "whatever it is you boys do. Tracy and I will see to supper."

Dolan leaned closer to Tracy. A sparkle twinkled in his eyes as he stared at his cousin's wife. "Don't listen to a thing she says."

"Scared?" Caitlyn teased.

"You have no idea," Dolan responded. The interplay between them seemed so natural—so close.

Caitlyn's laughter was magical, charming both men as they gazed at her adoringly and for some reason that pissed Tracy off. The intimate way Caitlyn sashayed toward Dolan, kissing his cheek was all she needed to see to know that the three of them were connected and she didn't mean through marriage.

Dammit. Now she felt miserable. Were they still an item? What about her and Rowdy's arrangement with him? A knot formed in her stomach. Maybe their time together had meant nothing. This really sucked.

Caitlyn threaded her arm through Tracy's and pulled her nearer. The closeness made her eyes widen. She tensed as the woman snuggled nearer. She was either awful friendly, accepting Tracy simply because Dolan did or—

Holy shit! Maybe they were swingers. Maybe Dolan brought her here to switch-play. Oh fuck. Maybe they planned a four-way for tonight's dessert.

God-ohGod-ohGod.

Maybe the men planned on watching the women go at it first. Her vivid imagination took wings, making her pulse race. Her heart beat like warring drums. Tracy had to admit she wanted to enhance her sexual experiences, but—

She stumbled, a sick feeling swimming in the pit of her belly. Cord was easy on the eyes, but she didn't find herself attracted to him. Although she didn't care about one's sexual preferences, she wasn't game to going down on a woman or vice versa while the man she desired looked on. She didn't want anyone but Dolan. Panic lodged in her throat. She didn't want to share Dolan.

It was true.

Although she felt attracted to Rowdy it was Dolan whom she dreamt of each night and who held her thoughts throughout the day. With just a touch he made her body tremble. Her heart squeezed with yearning.

"You okay?" Caitlyn asked patting her arm. Even before Tracy could answer she said, "Don't worry. I'll take care of you."

That's exactly what Tracy was worried about.

"I hope you like Cornish hens."

"What?" Tracy tried to jerk her wayward thoughts back to what Caitlyn was saying.

"Cornish hens and wild rice?" She smiled so prettily—and innocently. "It's a new recipe I'm trying. Do you like chicken?" She chatted on as they approached the house. "Please tell me you're not a vegetarian." Releasing Tracy's arm, she opened the screen door and stepped aside allowing Tracy to step inside. "So what do you think about our Dolan?"

Tracy hesitated, and then she turned around. *Our Dolan?* The words stuck in her craw. Jealousy crawled up her neck spreading heat across her cheeks.

"Oh my. I hope I haven't embarrassed you." After she entered the kitchen she let the screen door slam shut. "It's just we're so close. I—we care." Her voice softened.

Yeah. I bet you're close. Tracy forced an innocent smile. "Embarrassed? Me? Whatever for?" Thank God for high school acting classes. She took a deep breath, raising her chin slightly. "Dolan and I are associates. As you know we work together."

"Puleez." A canny grin told her the woman wasn't buying it. "I know Dolan. He's infatuated with you."

Now it was her turn to voice puleez. "It's professional respect."

"Oh honey, it's more than that." Caitlyn eyed her curiously. "But—" she shrugged, "whatever. So do you like Cornish hen?"

What the hell? They were back to chicken again?

"Yes. As a matter of fact, I love chicken." There. Enough

about the friggin' chicken. The juicy scent penetrated Tracy's senses. She didn't realize she was hungry until now.

"Wonderful." Bending, Caitlyn opened a cabinet and extracted a pan. "And the answer is no," she said standing and then heading for the sink.

Now what the hell was the woman talking about? "No?" Tracy bit, even though she knew she was being led down a blind path by the nose.

Caitlyn flashed a knowing grin over her shoulder. "We aren't sleeping together." She gave the knob a twist and watered cascaded into the pan. "Not since Cord and I got married."

The heaviness in her chest dissipated and relief that her assumptions about the night had been wrong took its place. But it was a backhanded relief. Dolan had slept with this woman, a fact that was like a rope around Tracy's tongue, making it difficult to speak. "I—Ah. I mean—" Laughter met her frustration.

Caitlyn turned off the faucet and placed a steamer basket inside the pan before placing it on the stove. "The men in this family love a good fuck. The more the merrier." She winked before reaching for the asparagus lying on the drainer and placing it inside the pan. "But once they settle down it's for good. They're one-woman men." She squared the lid on the pan and then wiped her hands on a towel lying on the counter. "Cord won't let another man touch me. If you're the right one for Dolan it'll be the same way."

That heaviness in Tracy's chest returned with a vengeance. Although she had thought she heard Dolan profess she was his, he had shared her yet again with Rowdy. Of course, she had asked for it, even craved it. The second time had been explosive. She had collapsed in his arms. After which he had mumbled something about an appointment, refused to eat lunch and left like his ass was on fire.

Igniting a flame beneath the pan, Caitlyn turned the stove down before facing her. "So who's Tracy Marx?"

Good question.

She went through the basic information about home, life and her love of animals choosing her current occupation. After she revealed the death of her father and her sister, Caitlyn sat on one of the kitchen chairs.

"Sit," she said, before adding, "I'm so sorry. Is your nephew with his father or your mother?"

Tracy pulled out a chair and sat. "No. Mom isn't well enough to take on a child and Sheldon's father isn't in the picture. My nephew will join me soon. I made a promise to my sister to care for him. I intend to keep it. Besides I love him like he is my own."

"So..." A perfectly plucked brow rose along with caution in her voice when she spoke again. "You've become an instant mother?"

Tears welled in Tracy's eyes, but she fought back the emotion. "Yes." It sounded funny even to her, but she was now Sheldon's mother.

"Does Dolan know?" Caitlyn must have realized the insinuation in her words, because she stuttered. "I-I mean—not that it would matter."

The hell it wouldn't. Clearly the woman sitting across from her thought differently.

"No. It hasn't come up in our conversations." Truthfully they hadn't done much talking when they got together. For the first time she understood how her sister must have felt. Second dates were rare once the man discovered a child was involved. The man who loved Tracy would also have to love the boy who meant so much to her.

Welcome to your new world, a small voice within her head said.

A smirk tugged at the corners of Cord's mouth. He shook his hand before his chest. "H-O-T."

Dolan hid a grin.

Walking side by side they headed in the direction of the pasture. "You didn't mention that she was drop-dead beautiful. Her hair is amazing, especially against that dress. And that voice." He paused. "Damn. It's enough to make a man come on the spot."

Pride squeezed Dolan's chest. Tracy did have the sexiest voice he had ever heard and she looked fantastic tonight when he picked her up. The soft flowing dress she wore hugged all the right places and showed enough leg, making him instantly hard. The emerald color made her hair glisten in contrast. For two cents he would have canceled dinner and instead spent the night peeling that dress off her.

Yet there was more to Tracy then a pretty face and a sexy body. She was intelligent and her down-home charm drew people like bees to honey. The confident way she handled not only their patients today, but their owners, was remarkable to watch. She had a casual way with people that drew their confidence. Of course, she had the training and knowledge to back her up. The staff was falling in love with her and that included him. He'd known it the first time he laid eyes on her.

They stopped before the fence. Cord placed a booted foot on the lower rung. "So?" he said looking out across the grassy field. Several thoroughbreds grazed quietly. The sun was setting in the west, creating streaks of reds, oranges and yellows across the sky.

Dolan rested his forearms on the fence. "So what?" He released a weighted sigh. Some day he would own a place like this—horses, cattle, a home, a wife and a family.

Cord cocked his head. "Last we talked she was a burr beneath your saddle blanket. Now I gather it's another blanket she's lying under." He hid the smile, but amusement danced in his eyes.

"Not much choice. Doc Zimmerman gave her a job."

"Bullshit." This time he did smile. "Who do you think you're talking to?"

"An asshole," Dolan said playfully.

"Don't think your sweet talk works on me." His expression grew serious. "So what's going on? Even Cait detected the heat between the two of you."

Dolan took his Stetson off and pushed his fingers through his hair. "I've fallen hard." He set his hat back upon his head. "Damn woman is always on my mind. She haunts me," he admitted without shame.

Cord wagged his head. "Yep. I know that feeling."

Silence stretched between them as they gazed blindly out across the land.

"So when do you think Taylor Tweeds will foal?" Cord asked watching the black mare with three white socks. Cait's mare Misty Dawn was also expecting a foal from Cord's stud.

"A week, maybe."

"Yep. Know that feeling," Cord repeated more to himself than Dolan. "Guess we'd better head back. Cait is trying out another new recipe."

"Is that good or bad?" Dolan asked as they headed toward the house.

"Depends. Either way I tell her it's great." Dolan saw love

reflecting in his cousin's bright eyes. "Would appreciate if you did the same."

So this is what love did to a man—made a liar out of him, killed his taste buds and gave him a cast iron stomach.

Dolan could live with that.

They entered the house and scents of roasting chicken and freshly baked bread touched his nose. His stomach growled and he prayed it was one of Cait's better days of cooking. He was hungry.

As they walked through the kitchen Cait had remodeled to go along with her new cooking interest, he marveled at the change she had wrought not only to his cousin, but the house. The western décor along with the bulky wood and leather furniture that he, Cord and his uncle had lived with for years was gone. Instead a more classical air rang in the furniture, curtains, carpet and accessories. Cait had left her mark in every room, including the dining room. A simple but classy chandelier hung above the elegant eight-seated dining table set for only four. Fresh flowers, china, not paper plates, crystal and silverware graced the table. Candlelight flickered softly.

Dolan took his hat off and hung it on the back of one of the chairs. He thought of his own home. It was cold, needing a woman's touch—Tracy's touch.

Her laughter stroked his ears and he turned to see her and Cait descending the stairs. As Tracy entered the room their eyes met and warmth surged through his veins.

"I was showing Tracy the rest of the house." Cait walked into Cord's arms.

"It's beautiful." Tracy stopped short of reaching him. There was something bothering her. He could feel the instant chill in the room.

"I'm afraid it's all her doing." Cord kissed his wife on the forehead. "She's dollified the house."

"Dollified? Is that a word? Maybe sissified. I know that's a real word." Dolan closed the distance between him and Tracy. "You okay?"

She nodded, but instinctively he felt her lie.

"Dolan." Caitlyn whined his name. "You don't like what I've done to the place?"

Cord touched his lips to hers. "He loves it. He's just jealous."

Had Cait said something to upset Tracy?

"Damn, Cord. She's got you wrapped right around her finger." His cousin didn't even try to dispute his jest.

Instead, he said, "Smells good. What culinary delight are we in for tonight?"

Cait beamed. "Cornish hens and wild rice."

"She's pretty high on chicken." Tracy smiled, but the gesture appeared strained.

"Ready to eat?" Cait stepped out of Cord's embrace. "Tracy, you and Dolan take a seat. Cord can help me in the kitchen."

Approaching the table, Dolan pulled out a chair for her.

"Thank you." She sat without speaking another word.

"Is something wrong?" He scooted out a chair and sat.

"Of course not."

He wanted to delve deeper, but Cord and Cait entered with four plates covered by silver domes. They set one in front of each of their empty seats, and then set the other plates before Dolan and Tracy. Cait lifted the dome and Dolan wanted to laugh, but suffocated the chuckle as it tickled his throat. The damn bird looked more like a pigeon. There wasn't an ounce of meat on its thighs.

"Mmmm. It looks great," he choked. Cait was oblivious to the laughter in his voice, but Tracy wasn't. She frowned at him. He winked and the hard lines in her face softened.

Cord was the first to take a chance on the cuisine before them. Everyone watched as he tore off a leg, placing the tiny thing into his mouth. Stripping the meat off the bone, he chewed. "This is really good, baby." He broke off the other leg and his wife grinned ear to ear.

Dolan ventured forward and cut into the breast. Liquid oozed from the chicken. He sliced a wedge and placed the meat on his tongue. Moist. Juicy. He chewed. Not half bad. Swallowing, he went for another bite.

"It's wonderful," Tracy said. "Isn't it, Dolan?"

Mouth full and chewing, he nodded.

The conversation was light as they ate. He discovered that Tracy loved horses, although she hadn't ridden in quite a while. Other than college this was the first time she'd lived away from home. She was already a little homesick, but anxious to establish herself in California. She cooked very little, but she hoped to rectify that.

"I can help," Cait offered. "I have tons of cookbooks."

"I can attest to that. We had to remodel the kitchen just to accommodate them." Cord released a dramatic sigh. He laughed, dodging his wife's hand as she playfully swung out at him.

"Ready for dessert?" she asked pushing to her feet. Tracy stood following her into the kitchen. Each carried two plates with pieces of chocolate cake as they stepped back into the room.

"Ah, honey you baked," Cord teased. "What's next—children?"

Both women briefly paused, quickly sharing glances before they continued to the table and set down the cake. Apparently Cord was unconscious of their hesitancy or the silence that followed because he said no more and eagerly began to devour his cake. The glow on Cait's face was gone as she took her seat. Even Tracy seemed a little peaked when she sat, placing her napkin back upon her lap.

As Dolan picked up his fork, he couldn't help but wonder, was Cait pregnant? How would his cousin feel about being a father? Would he want a child?

As steadfast bachelors, they had diligently practiced safe sex not only for health reasons, but to protect themselves from an unwanted pregnancy. Had marriage changed Cord's thoughts on children? Would he welcome a child into his life?

Dolan's gaze fell on Tracy as she took a bite of her dessert. Damn. She was beautiful. What would she look like heavy with his child? A tremor raked his spine. Lord. Where did that thought come from?

She caught him staring, "What?"

He set his fork down and placed his hand over hers, squeezing gently. "Ready to go?" He couldn't wait to get her home. Tonight she was all his.

Her eyes widened with surprise. "Uh." She looked from Cait to Cord. Grabbing her napkin from her lap, she placed it on her plate and started to push away from the table. "Yes. I guess if you are."

Cait's fork dropped against her plate, making a sharp sound. "Dolan, it's still early. Please stay a little longer. Besides you've barely touched your cake." Cord eased back in his chair, a roguish grin on his face. He knew exactly why Dolan wanted to leave.

Tonight's dessert was standing next to him. He looped his

arm around Tracy and felt her tense. "I know, but we both have to work tomorrow." Grasping ahold of his Stetson, he took it off the back of the chair and squared it on his head.

Tracy faced Cait. "I'm so sorry for not helping with the dishes."

"No worry," Cord interjected, standing to pull out his wife's chair as she stood. "I'll help her." He slapped her on the ass and she jumped.

The women chatted as they walked toward the door, while Cord and Dolan followed behind. Tracy's purse hung from the coat rack near the entrance. She retrieved it placing it over her shoulder.

"I like her," Cord murmured. "She'll be good for you."

Yeah. But how did anyone know who they would spend the rest of their lives with, Dolan wondered. "How did you know Cait was the one?"

A sappy expression fell across his cousin's face. "There wasn't a moment that she wasn't on my mind." He looked at her with such yearning. "I craved seeing her, touching her, but most of all I couldn't bear the thought of another man touching her." He paused, before adding, "Even you." Then he threw his arm around Dolan's shoulders. "Trust me. Don't let this one go."

No more was said as they joined the women. After saying their good-byes he and Tracy stepped outside into the moonlit night. He didn't hesitate taking her into his arms. She fit so right against him. The smell of her sweet perfume wrapped around his senses sending a bolt of hunger through his stomach straight to his cock, which jerked demandingly.

There was no denying it. He felt the perfection between them.

Lowering his head, he grew closer and her breath stuttered.

"God, you're beautiful." Kissing her forehead first, he caressed each of her eyelids and then her mouth. His lips tugged at hers, sipped from them. "Let me take you home and make love to you?" Before she could answer, he captured her mouth with his again.

Chapter Fourteen

Dolan's kiss was hungry, demanding. His mouth covered Tracy's, his tongue tangling with hers. He tasted of heat and the promise of an explosive night of hot sex. They would have one more night together before she revealed her secret.

Tonight she would tell him about Sheldon and end the most overwhelming connection she had ever felt with a man. Delaying the truth only complicated the situation. She was falling hard for him.

Was he aware of his own power, the desire he aroused within her?

Desperately she held on to him, not wanting to let him go even when the caress ended. Staring into his dark eyes, she felt lost in them. If only he had room in his heart to love her and accept the precious boy who needed a family—a father.

A shuddering breath brought her back to reality. Who was she kidding? They didn't even know each other. Whatever was happening between them had to be just a strong case of lust.

Besides Dolan was promiscuous. His reputation as a rake was well known. He wouldn't want a child any more than a wife.

She opened her mouth to speak but let it close without comment.

Just tell him. Get it over with.

His hands brushed up her back as he pressed his forehead to hers. "I've wanted to do that all night." A burst of nervous laughter caught her off guard. "No. That's a lie." His hand slipped to the small of her back, drawing her closer so that she felt his jean-clad arousal pressed hard to her belly. "I've wanted to peel that sexy green dress off of you. Throw you on the ground and fuck you." He grabbed her hand. "Come on, darlin', before I take you right here."

She swallowed past the emotion clogging her throat. As they walked to the truck, she looked into the starry night. Loving him tonight was selfish. She would pay for it with her heart, but she wanted one more night in this cowboy's arms.

He opened the truck door and light filled the cab. Easing closer, he pinned her between the seat and his hard body. His warm breath brushed over her face. "Take off your panties. I can't wait to feel that wet pussy."

Pulse leaping, she curled her fingers in his cotton shirt. "Dolan." Moisture dampened her thong. Arousal pulled at her breasts, making them feel heavy with need.

Desire shone in his eyes, but there was something more. It burned bright heating her blood. "Do it, darlin'." Low and sensual, his voice was like sparks igniting across her skin.

She wet her lips as excitement clenched low in her belly. "I—" Her body jerked against him.

He placed his palms on her thighs. "You want *me* to take them off don't you?" Smoothing his palms up her legs, he pushed the hem of her dress higher and higher.

"Dolan?" She breathed his name as cool air swept up her legs.

His thumbs slid past the elastic of her thong and paused. "What, baby?"

"What if they're looking out the window?" She didn't have to

168

say who; he knew she referred to Caitlyn and Cord.

A rumble rose from deep in his throat, clearly excited with the possibility. "Makes caressing you even hotter. Would you like them to watch me undress you, take you right here?"

His sinful words made her nipples pucker. Shards of electricity burst at the hardened peaks shooting down to her pussy. Like a rubber band her inner muscles tightened and loosened, preparing her for the moment she would have his cock buried inside her.

Tracy tossed her purse onto the floorboard of the truck. Placing her hands on his, she drove them downward, taking her thong with them.

He knelt, dragging the satiny material down her legs. "Oh yeah. Sweet, sweet pussy." She heard him inhale as she stepped out of the thong. He stood placing his palm on her heart-shaped mound. "Are you wet, darlin'?"

She was beyond wet and beyond caring if anyone watched. "Y-yes."

"Mmmm. Maybe I should check." As his finger slipped between her swollen folds, she gasped, hips bucking against his hand. "Just how I like you." Mouth against her ear, he whispered, "Slick and creamy."

He pumped his thick finger in and out of her, once, twice. Her thighs widened on their own accord. It felt so good. She held on to his shirt, afraid she'd fall if she let go. When he extracted his finger, she whimpered. Strong hands gripped her by the waist raising her. Cool leather met her ass when he sat her upon the truck seat.

"Ready to go?" he asked, releasing her.

Oh hell no.

Leaning back on a palm, she whined, "Dolan, don't leave

me like this." Spreading her legs, her dress fell between them hiding the very area where his gaze was pinned. "I ache for you." With her free hand she began to inch her dress up. "Lick my pussy."

His eyes darkened as he shoved her dress all the way up to expose her sex. "Damn. Woman, you fuck with my mind and body."

Every muscle in her body tensed. The expression on his face was like that of a man thirsty for a taste of what she offered. She had never seen anything as erotic as he watched his fingers slip through the juices that eased from her sex. When he closed the distance between his gorgeous mouth and the pulse between her thighs she held her breath.

As his tongue slid over her slit, the air in her lungs released upon a moan. Warm. Wet. He stroked her tender flesh, over and over, flicking her clit on every pass. But it wasn't enough, she needed more. Pulling her legs up, sandals flat on the seat, she let her bent knees fall apart. "Now, baby, suck me."

He tore off his hat and tossed it in the backseat. "Fuck." His strong hands slipped beneath her ass lifting her hips. "I ought to spank you for teasing me."

"No teasing." Her breathing was laboured, heavy in her chest. "I'm yours for the taking." God save her. She would give him her heart if only he wanted it. For now she'd take whatever he offered.

There was a pregnant pause. A moment where all he did was look at her. Then the unthinkable happened. He lowered her legs, pushing them inside the truck. Like a rock her heart fell heavy into her stomach.

His jaws were so taut that the tendons in his neck bulged. He pushed his fingers through his hair. "I won't take you like this." His tone edged on anger.

"Dolan, I'm—" The apology she started to offer caught in her throat as the truck door slammed shut. Darkness folded around her as the light blinked out.

For a mere second she couldn't breathe. Memories of her husband's reprimanding voice rang in her ears. *You're sick*, he'd say when she wanted to try something different in or outside of bed. Night after night she had sat in the dark alone—crying—unfulfilled and afraid that something had to be wrong with her.

Dammit. A shudder racked her spine as she exhaled. She wouldn't feel guilty for asking for what she wanted. Not any more. There wasn't anything wrong with her. Besides, Dolan had started it, asking her to remove her thong. She watched him walk around the truck, her anger growing with each of his heavy steps.

Pushing back her hair, she inhaled, waiting until he climbed into the truck. The engine roared to life. "Take me like what?" Her voice shook. "You'll fuck me with your friend, but truck sex is too kinky for the bad boy of Santa Ysabel?"

He snapped his startled stare to hers. "What?" There was an awkward moment of silence. "Darlin'," his voice grew tender, "I want you to myself, in a bed—my bed."

Well that was friggin' great. Her skin felt like it shrank two sizes too small. She had made a total fool of herself. He must think she was some whack-job.

The headlights of a passing car lit the cab. She saw his broad grin just before the cab went dark again.

"Bad boy of Santa Ysabel?" There was amusement in his tone.

If Tracy could crawl under the seat she would have.

"That title actually belongs to Cord, or did before he got married. As for kinky, baby, you haven't seen kinky."

Why did it feel as if she had just opened a can of worms?

Something was brewing. Dolan didn't know exactly what it was, but her moods tonight had made more flip-flops than a fish out of water. He still hadn't figured out why she was so quiet at Cord's. Her recent spark of anger was something that came out of nowhere. All he wanted to do was make love to her the right way, not like some rutting animal.

"So," he glanced at her before looking back to the road ahead. "Are you going to tell me what's up?"

She licked her lips and stared out into the dark. "Nothing."

"Wrong answer." He had learned that "nothing" meant "something" to a woman. Reaching across the console, he placed his hand on her knee. "Did Cait say something to upset you?"

"No. Of course not." Was it just his imagination or did her voice shake?

"Does Cord know she's pregnant?"

Tracy faced him, shadows hiding her expression when a car passed, flooding the cab with light. "She's pregnant?" He saw surprise widen her eyes. Had he misread their reaction during dessert?

"She's not?" he asked.

Her brows tugged down. "Uh?"

"Forget it." He removed his hand and gripped the steering wheel. "I thought— Well, it's just that after Cord mentioned children both of you seemed to—"

Oh fuck. His fingers tightened around the steering wheel. He turned to look at her as the blood in his veins thickened. "Are you pregnant?" Uneasy laughter met his delicate question.

"For heaven sakes." She shook her head as if to say he was

a dumbass. "No, I'm not pregnant." Another moment of silence followed. "How about you? Pregnant?"

He felt the sheepish grin that pulled at the corner of his mouth. "Nah. I'm good."

"I'm glad we cleared the air on that subject."

He couldn't tell if she was teasing or meant it. "So why did you lose it when I suggested a soft bed instead of a truck bed?" The way she squirmed in her seat revealed she was uncomfortable with the subject.

Moments passed before she spoke. "My husband." She cleared her throat. "Ex-husband, ridiculed me every time I suggested any position other than missionary style. Guess he was old fashioned because there was only one way to have sex, me flat on my back and him on top. His idea of foreplay was a kiss and a pinch." Dolan thought he heard a tear in her voice.

Sonofabitch. Why were men insensitive to a woman's needs? It took very little to listen and discover what made her purr.

Hell. That's what he enjoyed the most about meeting a new woman, getting to know her and her body.

Yet the circumstances hadn't allowed him the opportunity to get to know Tracy. Instead he went straight to her bed every time he could, which didn't say much for him.

"Tracy, I'm sorry."

She stared out the window. "It doesn't matter."

"It does to me. I just thought—" That he would show her how much she meant to him by loving her in a way she deserved. "How long were you married?"

"Too long." The shortness in her response said the conversation was over.

"Marx is your married name?"

173

"No maiden. I didn't want anything from that man." Her obvious distaste answered any questions as to whether there were any lingering feelings. They rode in silence for a while until he turned north instead of south.

"Where are we going?" she asked.

"My house." Very seldom did he take a woman home. It was his safe haven. Yet he wanted this woman in his home and his bed.

"But I have to work tomorrow. I don't have any clothes, make-up—"

"I'll get you home in time for you to freshen up and change. Tonight you're mine. Now take your sandals off."

"Why?"

"Foreplay, darlin'. I do know its value." In fact, he was getting hard just thinking about her lack of panties. He couldn't wait to part her thighs and sink into her warmth. "Now take your sandals off and put your feet on the dashboard."

"Dolan—"

"I want you hot for me when I get you in my arms." He reached down and adjusted himself. Damn. He wanted this woman.

She toed off her shoes and placed her feet together on his dashboard

"Spread 'em." He glanced in the rear-view mirror, but when he looked back at her he was pleased. She had inched her feet apart. "Push your dress up around your waist."

"Dolan," she breathed his name. "Someone will see me."

"Maybe—maybe not." His voice was gravelly. His cock jerked, growing harder. The truth was they had just pulled off the main street onto a private road. No one would see her, but the thought would heighten her arousal, make her even hotter.

He eased up on the gas pedal slowing down. "Now touch yourself."

Silence filled the cab and then she moaned, a low breathy sound.

Envisioning her long slender fingers pushing in and out, stroking her sensitive skin was too much. He reached down and unfastened his belt and jeans, unzipping them to ease his discomfort. The thought of her touching herself made him horny as hell. He had to take a look.

When he switched on the cab lights, her eyelids flew wide. Surprise mingling with lust burned in their depths as a tight cry slipped from her mouth. She jerked back her hand nestled between her legs and scrambled to pull down her dress.

"Damn, darlin', don't stop."

Her gaze darted nervously around. "I can't believe you did that." Embarrassment dotted her cheeks. She was so adorable. Playful and forward one minute, then shy and timid the next.

He could see by her frown she didn't appreciate his chuckle. "We're on a private road. No one will see you but me. Come on, Tracy, I want to watch your fingers move all over that pink, swollen flesh."

She glanced around to verify the fact. The scowl she wore faded into a mischievous grin. She angled her body toward him and his throat tightened. "So you want a show." Her sexy voice was liquid heat sizzling through his veins.

"A show?" His cock firmed even more. His fingers gripped the steering wheel.

She slid her tongue seductively between her lips. Bending one knee, she planted her foot on the edge of the console. The other leg she stretched, widening her thighs and taking her time, before she placed her foot against the dashboard. All the while she kept both hands strategically placed between her thighs to hold her dress down and rob him of a peek of what he wanted to see.

He swallowed hard. "Raise your dress, darlin'. Show me that pussy."

Looking at him through half-shuttered eyelids, she shook her head.

A sudden bump warned him that he had strayed off the road. He jerked the wheel, pulling the truck back on track. He needed to pay more attention to driving and less on the temptress trying to distract him.

One of her hands disappeared beneath her dress and a pang exploded in his groin. "Fuck. Don't do this to me, darlin'. Let me see."

Ignoring him, she arched her back, lips parting on an "Oh." She raised her hips, thrusting against her hand. Exhaling, she hummed, "Ahhh... Feels so good."

Dolan's grip on the steering wheel whitened his knuckles. His cock had pushed past his zipper and curved angrily against his belly. A pulse radiated through his balls. Even his hips began to keep the pace to the movement of her hand.

Her breathing had become choppy pants. The fact that she was aroused, wanted to touch herself for him, was fucking hot. A trembling hand pushed the silky material up her legs, inch by inch.

"Yeah, darlin', higher." Dolan nearly lost the truck again when he swerved into a ditch. "Fuck." Once again he righted the vehicle as the lights of his house came into view. Instead of slowing down he hit the gas.

Gravel popped as he reached the pebbled driveway and pulled the truck to a screeching halt. He didn't shut off the engine. No. His entire attention was on the woman whose bottom half lay completely exposed.

Tracy's breasts were heavy. Her nipples rasping lightly against the bodice of the dress with each ragged breath. Eyes dark as the night watched her with an intensity that sent a tremor up her spine and into her hands. Even her legs quivered. She was so close to coming that she didn't dare go near her clit. Touching that spot would set her off like a keg of gunpowder.

Breathe. She made an "O" with her mouth and released the air from her lungs. Focusing her fingertips on her swollen folds, she slid them over the slick flesh.

Never taking his stare off her of pussy, Dolan drew nearer, draping his body over the console. His fingers circled her ankle and for a mere second she thought he might taste her, but he didn't.

She wanted him to lick her—but not, as she entered the point where she hung on the precipice. The dreamy place that consumed her senses—her body felt so good that climaxing would be blissful but end the moment of rapture. The motion of her fingers slowed. Hearing consisted of nothing but the rapid beat of her heart echoing in her ears.

Leaning forward, he removed her hand and blew a warm breath over her moist skin. She closed her eyes, fighting a losing battle. But it was his tongue, wet and warm, wrapping around the swollen bud that shattered her control. As he sucked long and hard, her body ignited, raining pleasure down upon her. She didn't even try to restrain the scream that tore from her diaphragm. Every muscle inside clenched. A heat wave surged over her with each delicious throb. She prayed it would go on and on, but it didn't. Too soon it was over.

Releasing a deep sigh, she opened her heavy eyelids to see male satisfaction staring back at her.

"How's that for foreplay?" He placed a kiss against her sex.

Like every time they came together, she had never felt as sated as she did when she was with him. "Hmmm. Perfect."

Sitting up, he brushed his palms up and down her legs before he reached for the keys. The engine died and the light blinked out. The door moaned as he opened it, climbed out and then swung it close. As he walked around the truck, she righted herself, fumbling around in the darkness to find her sandals and purse. She was slipping her shoes on when he opened her door and pulled her into his arms.

Their lips touched. His kiss was tender. She tasted herself on him. The scent and musky flavor was arousing, pleasing. "Stay with me tonight?" The yearning in his voice made her answer stick in her throat.

Thankfully he couldn't see moisture filled her eyes. As her body slid down his, her feet touching the gravel driveway, she turned away to shield the raging emotions that rolled in from out of nowhere.

How could she have fallen for him so quickly? This was ridiculous. Lord knows they had experienced roadblocks one after another, but for some unknown reason they were drawn to each other. That alone told her that if their relationship was to be it would be. With that in mind she would take what he offered tonight. Tomorrow she would lay her cards on the table and pray he wouldn't walk away.

Chapter Fifteen

As Dolan held Tracy in front of his house, he waited for an answer that didn't materialize. He had never asked a woman to stay over. His home was his sanctuary. Yet he wanted—no needed—her to spend night. Moonlight fell across her beautiful face before she turned away. Were those tears or a trick of the night?

She cleared her throat. "It's so quiet."

Adjusting his hold, he slid an arm around her shoulders. "That's the thing I like about this place, that and no city lights." They started walking toward his three bedroom country home with a porch that wrapped completely around it. "Sometimes at night or early morning I sit on the swing and just listen to the sounds of nature or inhale the sweet scent of hay rolling off of one of Cord's fields." Even now he could smell the alfalfa on the breeze that stirred around them. But the grassy aroma was nothing compared to the light scent of Tracy on his mustache. He ran his tongue along his upper lip, tasting her again. Her expression of ecstasy as she touched herself in the truck was still embedded in his mind.

As they approached the stairs leading to his house, he released her. Her sandals slapped the wooden steps as she climbed and then waited for him to follow. The old swing creaked, swaying in the wind as currents of air danced a gathering of leaves around the floor making a scraping sound. Leading the way to the door, he fished out his house key from his jeans. After he opened the door, he moved aside and let her enter. Grappling in the dark for the light switch, his fingertips touched it. With a click, light filled the room.

She blinked as he squinted.

Tracy looked around the small living room. "Dolan, this is so cozy."

Did that mean it was small or comfortable? For some reason it meant a lot to him that she liked his home.

Mrs. Cartwright had helped him to decorate the house. She had given him the crocheted afghan across the tan leather couch. Hell. She had even provided the two end tables on each side of the sofa, and the wooden rocking chair sitting near the old fireplace. The valance that accented the large window seat looking over acres of land was also hers. A modest size flat screen television hung from the wall that was adorned with western art—art provided by Cord when Cait redecorated. Tile went throughout the house with throw rugs in every room.

Still, the prettiest thing in the house was Tracy. Amazingly, she looked like she belonged here. She handed him her purse as he removed his hat, hanging both of them on the coat rack near the door.

"Thank you," she said.

He took her into his arms, unable to resist her touch.

Would their night together be a moment of rushed sex before she demanded he take her home? Or would she stay and allow him to love her the way she deserved?

He lowered his head and captured her mouth. Gently he stroked her lips with his tongue, nudging between them to gain entrance. Her lips parted and he pushed past them to taste her. Their tongues met, tangled and smoothed up and down one another. Tightening his hold, he leaned his head to one side and deepened the caress. Hot and urgent, he couldn't get enough as he devoured her.

Her arms snaked around his neck. He shuffled his feet pushing her back against the wall. Looping his hands beneath her knees he raised her. She locked her legs around his waist. His palms gripped her bare ass, reminding him she wore no panties. His cock went from semi-hard to rock-hard in nanoseconds.

As he pressed his hips to her center, his jeans slid across her pussy. She cried out and he swallowed her whimper.

"I need you naked," he groaned between kisses.

She arched her neck. "Yes." He savored the saltiness of her skin and inhaled the light flowery perfume she chose to wear tonight.

Using his body to brace her against the wall, he knotted his fingers into the hem of her dress and worked it up, forcing her to release the hold she had on his neck. As he pulled the garment over her head, she gave him a heart stopping smile and replaced her arms around his neck. The dress slipped from his fingertips to drop to the floor and her sandals followed.

His gaze stroked her body. "So beautiful. I can't wait to fuck you."

She released her ankles, allowing her body to slide down the wall until her feet touched the floor. The come-hither look she gave him was all he needed.

Moving away, he sat on the edge of the couch and quickly removed his boots and socks. As he stood he pulled his T-shirt over his head and then reached into his pocket, extracting a condom. Pushing his jeans to his ankles he stepped out of them. Without pausing, he rolled the latex over his erection.

Damn. She was beautiful.

Wavy red hair fell down past her shoulders. Full breasts begged to be fondled and touched.

He closed the distance between them, his palms cupping her face. Gazing into her dreamy blue-green eyes, emotions he had never felt before assailed him. Every inch of him felt tied into a knot. Lord, help him. If this was love, it was the most complete and most fucked-up feeling he had ever felt.

Leaning into her, he sipped from her mouth needing more but wanting the night to last forever. "Move in with me." Her bright stare was nothing to the shock he felt coursing through his body. Fear. Anticipation. Threads of hope wrapped around him like chains holding him in a web of expectation.

"Dolan. I—"

He kissed her again not wanting to hear the rejection building in her tone. When the caress ended she appeared weary.

"Don't answer now. Just consider it." He raised her in his arms and carried her through the room, down the hall to the master bedroom.

Dolan liked his comfort and he had splurged on a massive king-size bed. The comforter was pillow soft. He laid her upon it and marveled at how right she looked lying on his bed.

Misty-eyed, she stared at him.

He felt his confidence slip. Dammit. He was moving too fast. Yet every fiber in his body told him this was right. Her. Him. He just needed more time.

Neither spoke as he crawled upon the bed beside her. Resting his head on a palm, he smoothed his other hand across her firm belly. She was warm, soft. "You feel so good."

She opened her arms. "Come here." Like a puppet on a string he fell into them. The minute her arms folded around him he sighed. They lay there for only a moment before she said, "We need to talk."

He eased up placing some distance between them to see sorrow reflecting in her eyes. But he didn't want to deal with it—not now. "Not tonight."

More time whispered in his head as he wedged his knee between her legs spreading her wide.

"Tonight is for lovin'—tomorrow talking." He swallowed hard, hoping she would yield. "Okay?"

She inhaled a ragged breath. "Dolan?"

Trepidation slid over his skin. He brushed back her hair, knowing that if she wanted to talk then talk they would. If he had to, he'd admit his feelings for her and beg if necessary. "Yes, darlin'?"

"Love me." Her voice sounded so small with an air of hopelessness that twisted his gut.

"I plan to. All. Night. Long."

Tracy didn't really want to talk tonight either. She wanted to believe in happy endings—she wanted to believe that this man would accept her no matter her situation.

Moving to his knees, he raised her hips and stuffed a pillow beneath them. Positioning her, his hands were warm on her skin. As he stepped forward, his cock pressed against the pulse between her thighs. She closed her eyes preparing for the moment of bliss. With one thrust he parted her slit and slipped deep inside. Instant gratification filled her with awe.

"Yes." The single word came out a hiss of pleasure.

Raising her arms, she started to reach for him, pull him closer, but he took control. Intertwining his fingers with hers, he pinned them to each side of her head. He rocked his hips against hers, back and forth, the gentle pace so sensual it heightened her senses. He eased out leaving her with an empty filling. Before she could object, he swayed forward driving deep to stroke the back of her sex. Over and over, he made love to her with such tenderness she wondered if her heart would be the same after tonight.

Her eyelids fluttered open. The intensity of his stare as he watched his cock move in and out of her body was arousing. Her breasts grew heavier, nipples tingling, as moisture released between her thighs. Slick. Hot. Their bodies swayed in perfect harmony.

"Mine," he growled. The throaty avow wrapping around her heart.

If only it were true.

Emotions rose so quickly she felt like she was drowning. She gasped. "I need to touch you." She needed to take control, stop herself from falling deeper into the spell he was weaving around her.

He shook his head.

"Please," she begged just as he angled his hips, stroking a sensitive area that triggered a series of ripples throughout her body. "Oh God."

"No." It was a strained demand. "Not." His jaws clenched as his brows furrowed. "Yet." He pushed the last word through his teeth. Dragging in a deep breath, his chest seemed to expand.

She flexed her inner muscles to hold back the orgasm beating for release.

"Fuck." His grip tightened. He raised his head, his hot gaze meeting hers. "Now. Come for me."

Responding to his command, the fire that simmered inside her exploded. At the same time he jerked against her, threw back his head and cried out.

The moment was spectacular, beyond anything she could imagine. Their bodies were in sync, pulsing to the same rhythm, as their orgasms washed over them with the ferocity of a tempest. A whirling mass of sensations caught in the motion, bringing them closer and closer together. They breathed simultaneously. Even the beat of their hearts melded into one.

Their climaxes crested and he released her hands, easing atop her so that nothing stood between them. Strong arms held her close as the final note played, leaving a light hum across her skin. She basked in the aftermath, breathing in his masculine scent and reveling in its potency.

The scream of a telephone ripped her out of the dreamy state that had embraced her. Was it his cell phone or hers? She looked around the room for a clock. It had to be close to eleven. A call this late meant an emergency.

"Fuck," he moaned again but didn't move. "I'm sorry." After two more rings, he released her pushing into a sitting position. Weaving his fingers through his hair, he got to his feet.

Moving to the side of the bed, she saw the red light of his telephone blinking against his belt. He picked up his jeans and silenced the telephone by flipping open the cover and pressing it to his ear.

"Crane." Quietly he listened to the person on the other end. "Okay. Yeah. I'll be there in about twenty minutes." He snapped the telephone closed and hung it on his belt. Peeling the condom off, he tossed it in the waste basket before using a tissue from atop the dresser to clean up. Without hesitating he reached for his jeans and pulled them over his legs and hips and fastened them.

She got to her feet. "I'll go with you?"

He cocked a brow. "In your sexy little dress? How do you

think that'll look to Kevin Laski?"

"Dunguard?" She remembered the horse's bleeding condition.

Dolan nodded. "The man is a sonofabitch." He pushed his arms through the sleeves of his shirt.

"I'll call Rowdy and see if he can pick me up and take me home."

"Stay here." He slipped on his socks. "I'll try to get back as soon as I can."

"You and I both know you may be all night. I need to be in the office at eight tomorrow morning."

"This is all fucked up."

"No. It's the life both of us chose." She eased into his arms and he kissed her quickly.

"Sorry I have to leave. I'll call Rowdy for you on the way out." He flipped open his cell phone as he headed for the door.

"Thank you." She doubted he heard her as he disappeared through the open door.

In seconds she was alone. She looked around the room. Across from the bed was a matching highboy. A dark green runner that matched the bed's comforter adorned the bureau. Atop the dresser was a picture of a woman and man holding a young boy—Dolan? His small arms were locked tightly around his father's neck. They looked so happy, the perfect family. On each side of the photograph were individual pictures of who she assumed were his mother and father.

Emotion dampened Tracy's eyes. There was so much in common between Dolan and Sheldon. Both had lost their parents at such a young age. She wrapped her arms around her naked shoulders as goose bumps rose across her skin. Would he see the resemblance? Would it make a difference? Mentally, she shook the thought away and went on a hunt for her dress.

The house was quiet as she drifted through the hall into the living room. Locating her dress on the floor, she picked it up and slithered into it, the soft material caressing her sensitive skin. She took a second to take in her surroundings as she spied her sandals and picked them up. He had made every attempt to make an empty shell of a house a home, from the blanket thrown across the sofa to the area rug before the fireplace. Even a rocking chair sat expectantly. Yet it still felt cold, almost unlived in.

Again sadness crept into her thoughts. Had his mother rocked him as a child? What had he been like?

Restlessly, she started to walk through the house, trying to find hints of his childhood. Other than the pictures of his parents in his bedroom, there were six pictures total of his uncle, Cord and Dolan, which apparently summed up his entire life. The fact there were no women's pictures both saddened and appeased her. No one had captured his heart enough for him to want to make a memory of their relationship.

Booted steps made her turn. Rowdy stood in the doorway of Dolan's living room with an expression she couldn't read. He didn't speak, just stared at her for longer then was comfortable.

Hand against the wall, she braced herself, slipping her feet in her sandals. "What?"

"You like him?" Of course, he referred to Dolan, but she pretended otherwise.

"Him?" she asked.

He stepped through the doorway into the room. "Do you really want to play this game?" There was something different in his solemn tone and expression that made her pause. She'd never seen a serious side of him before.

"Yes. I mean no games and yes I like him, but—" Damn.

This was hard. She bit her bottom lip trying to find the words to express what she had to say. When Sheldon arrived the triangle between her, Dolan and Rowdy would have to end. Hell. Whatever was happening between her and Dolan would end as well. In reality she had to think about a more stable relationship, one that would offer Sheldon a home—a family—a father and mother.

She took a hard look at Rowdy. Was he the right man?

A frown darkened his expression as if he read her mind. "It's okay. I know I'm not the one for you."

Confusion narrowed her eyes. Was he breaking it off with her? How fucking ironic was that?

Even as a mocking laugh rose in her throat, so did a sense of failure and self-reproach. It made a direct hit to her heart. She swallowed, trying to push away thoughts of her ex-husband and broken marriage.

Damn. Why did this always happen?

He began to walk toward her and every tendon in her body grew taut. He stopped when he stood before her. Thankfully, he didn't try to touch her, but he did use the endearment he had called her ever since they'd met. "Baby, we've had fun together."

But? she thought sarcastically, yet held her tongue. Instead her backbone stiffened, preparing for the next turn of the knife.

What the hell is wrong with you? This is the answer to your problem.

True. Yet it didn't take away the shot to her ego.

This time he touched her face, tracing a finger along her jaw line. "Let's face it." His smile didn't reach his eyes. In fact, she could swear she saw pain. "We don't have the heat that exists between you and Dolan."

Was it that obvious?

"Rowdy, it's just sex." She found herself saying but not believing and neither did he.

He cocked a brow. "Any fool can see the chemistry between the two of you. You'd have to be blind not to see you mean more to him than a quick fuck. I know Dolan. We've shared women before, but you're different. Hell. He actually growled at me when I attempted to kiss you the last time we were together."

Now that he mentioned it, Dolan had seemed agitated. Tracy had chalked it up to the fact he had several more appointments that afternoon. But as she thought more about it he had become possessive and demanding.

Cait's earlier comment touched Tracy's mind. *"But once they settle down it's for good. They're one-woman men."*

Dolan had asked her to move in with him. Could that mean—

The glimmer of hope she allowed herself to feel vanished when a shadow crept across Rowdy's face.

"It's time for me to move on." As if he suddenly became aware of his melancholy he flashed a grin that appeared a little too tight to be believable, and then he winked. "Let me take you home before I change my mind."

He tried to grasp her hand, but she pulled away. "What if he doesn't want me?" Insecurities rushed in to meet her. Rowdy was walking away. What if Dolan did the same?

As tears surfaced, Rowdy hauled her into his arms. Comfort surrounded her as it always did when he attempted to ease her mind.

"Baby, he'd be an idiot not to love you."

She prayed he was right. "What about us?" she asked. "Will we still be friends, even if Dolan doesn't—?" She choked on the thought, unable to complete her sentence.

"I'll always be here for you," he promised, giving her a little squeeze. "Who knows, maybe some day I'll find a woman—" He stopped abruptly. "C'mon, let me take you home."

"Rowdy, is everything okay?"

He gifted her with one of his fabulous smiles. "Of course."

As he ushered her out the door, Tracy knew he wasn't all right. Was it a woman?

"Rowdy?"

"Hmmm?"

"I'll always be here for you, too, if you ever want to talk."

He stopped, pulling her into his arms. She felt him tense. Heard the breath he sucked in. Pressing his lips to her forehead, he whispered, "Thank you." Then as quickly as he had embraced her he released her, opened the truck door, and she slid inside. She watched as he walked around the vehicle and got in, refusing to look at her as he started the engine.

As he pulled out of Dolan's driveway, Tracy knew there was more to Rowdy then what he allowed others to see. Would she ever really know him?

Maybe—maybe not.

Chapter Sixteen

The weekend had been as chaotic as the first three days of the week. Tracy opened the supply room door and slipped inside, the door closing behind her. Dolan's schedule had been complicated by a conference, which meant she had picked up the slack. She stared at the rows of supplies on the metal shelves. Everything seemed to have a place, except for what she was looking for. Gauze pads. She ran her gaze along the top shelf.

The work this past week had been invigorating and rewarding. She dropped her gaze to the second row of shelves. "Syringes, cotton balls..." Her mind drifted as she continued to list the supplies in her head instead of out loud.

Dolan had been right. The staff was wonderful to work with. Dr. Zimmerman was a wealth of knowledge. She had met so many influential people. Some were receptive to a female vet—some not.

But she wouldn't give up.

Her gaze dropped to the final row and began to scan it.

The only real problem about this last week—she had missed Dolan something terrible. The nights he hadn't called left her fidgety and on edge. Of course there was that other issue. Sheldon. The opportunity to speak to him about her nephew never seemed to present itself. At least she felt good about the caregiver she had hired.

She pivoted around and spied several boxes in the corner. As she headed toward them, she pondered how comfortable she felt with the mother of two. Mandy's children were around Sheldon's age. Plus she provided an activity schedule that met with Tracy's approval. The location was convenient, within several blocks of the office. She would be able to take Sheldon to lunch from time to time.

Leaning over a box, she ripped the tape off. Rummaging through the contents, she nearly jumped out of her skin when someone slid behind her and pressed against her ass. Strong hands gripped her hips, held her close so that she could feel that "someone" was all male. Relief flittered through her. She hadn't seen Dolan since she arrived at the office this morning.

There was so much she wanted—needed to say to him. Sheldon would be arriving Saturday and she had to find out what that meant to their relationship. But for now, she wanted to feel his arms around her.

Easing back into him as she stood, she asked, "So how was the conference—" Her voice froze as she inhaled a clean woodsy scent. Everything inside her screamed, *Oh God. No.* The familiar cologne told her immediately who held her and it wasn't Dolan. Looking over her shoulder, she was greeted with a smirk stretched across Zach's smug face.

The damn man had the nerve to smooth his palms to her waist, holding her immobile when she tried to step away. "Expecting someone else, Dr. Marx?" His arms folded around her waist, pulling her nearer. His peppermint breath brushed her neck, sending chills across her skin.

Dammit. This could only happen to her. Would he tell his father about her and Dolan? "Mr. Zimmerman—"

"Zach." He caressed her cheek with his. "Call me Zach."

"Mr. Zimmerman, this is inappropriate." Her heart raced a mile a minute as she stood perfectly still, unsure of how to break from his hold without making a scene. "Please release me." Her voice trembled, giving away her nervousness.

"You don't really want me to let you go? Now do you?" His tone was mocking. Something warm and wet against her skin made her struggle. "Hush, doll." He licked a path up her neck.

"Stop this minute," she demanded, but was thrown off guard when he turned her in his arms. She struggled to catch her footing, giving him the opportunity to pull her to him.

He was stronger, controlling her as she slammed against his chest, close enough that their noses were a breath away. "Clearly you haven't asked the same of Crane."

What the fuck? His words lit the fuse to her anger. Who the hell did he think he was?

"Get your hands off me." This time her voice held all the fury his comment conjured. Instead of letting her go he lowered his head, pressing his mouth to hers.

A moment of shock held her in its steely grip. Before she could draw back her hand and slap the shit out of the asshole, the door flew open.

Dolan stood like an avenging angel in the doorway. Rage burned in his eyes. The red-hot glare he pinned on Zach was enough to melt iron.

Yet Zach appeared unruffled. The sonofabitch smiled. Hugging her closer like a lover, he said "Joining us?" A whimper of distress surfaced as she pressed her palms on his shoulders and shoved, but he held her tightly. "I bet you've discovered how much our little doctor enjoys threesomes." He snuggled against her neck. "Don't you, honey?"

Dolan jerked his hot stare to her. Denial stuck in her throat. She felt her eyelids widen in disbelief as his accusing

193

Mackenzie McKade

stare struck her like arrows to the heart. She gasped.

He believed Zach?

Before she could find her voice, he turned his back on her, and the door closed behind him. She didn't even get the opportunity to explain. Resentment and outrage hit her at the same time another pang in her chest resulted.

"That's Crane." Zach's insulting tone had returned. "Love 'em and leave 'em." He paused briefly. "Ahhh... Did you think you'd be different?" He looked into her misty eyes. "You did. Well, I'm here now." He lowered his head, aiming for her lips, as she thrust her knee upward.

Blood drained from his face. His painful groan revealed she had hit her mark. His body jerked as he released her. Hugging his family jewels, his knees buckled before he crumbled like a day-old cookie to the floor.

God only knows what came over her. Instead of turning around and beating the living crap out of the bastard, she ran out of the supply room. Yanking her head from left to right and back again, she stared down every hallway, desperate to find Dolan.

Dressed in green scrubs, Beth was coming out of the surgical room. She pushed her glasses up her nose, holding an x-ray she studied in her other hand.

Tracy pulled to a stop before her. "Crane," she breathed his name. "Have you seen him?"

She shook her head. Her expression filled with concern. "Is something wrong, Dr. Marx?"

Tracy tried to smile, hiding the fact her pulse was racing out of control. Tears hid just behind her eyelids. Damn. She had never let a man get to her like Dolan did. "No. I just need to catch him before—" She caught a glimpse of Courtney as she turned around a corner. "Courtney?"

The young blonde reappeared into the hallway. "Yes, Dr. Marx."

"Have you seen Dr. Crane?"

The young technician released a nervous chuckle. "Left out the back door like his tail was on fire. Emergency I guess, but he looked mad enough to spit nails. Do you want me to get him on the telephone for you?"

"No." Maybe Tracy could catch him. Moving hastily, she headed for the back entrance. The screech of tires met her as she opened the door. Dolan's truck fishtailed as he gassed it.

Gone, whispered through her mind. She swallowed hard, fighting back emotion clawing at her throat.

Who was she kidding? Like Zach said, it was just a matter of time. A leopard didn't change it spots. Dolan was a steadfast bachelor. He lived in the fast line. She couldn't keep up with him. Besides there was much more at stake here—her career and Sheldon.

Swallowing hard, she struggled to pull herself together. Wiping angrily at tears, she took one more look down the road, and then she walked back to the building.

Inside, she tried to remember what she'd been doing before her world spun out of control. "Gauze pads," she said aloud. She had used the last one on her most recent client, a curious cat with a two-inch laceration on its head. Hopefully, he had learned that there were some places that didn't need to be explored. She'd have to remember that in the future.

Dolan slammed his hand on the steering wheel. He still hadn't come to grips with catching Tracy in Zach's arms. His pain had turned to anger. For some damn reason he felt betrayed. Yeah. It was true that she had never promised herself to him. She hadn't even committed to moving in with him. The last week had been hell wondering what she was doing. Now he knew.

"Dumbshit," he chastised. Here he was opening his home and more importantly his heart to her, while she was finding other entertainment. Damn it to hell. How could he have been so wrong about her?

Bring. Bring. He glanced down at his cell phone. He was in no mood to talk to anyone. The insistent ringing made him extract the telephone from his belt and look at the caller ID. Cord's name flashed in green letters. He flipped the cover open and pressed it to his ear.

"It's time," his cousin said with eagerness in his voice. "How close are you?"

Dolan looked around in a daze. He had left the office in a blinding rage, having no idea where he was going, only that he had to get away. Culver's ranch appeared in the distance and he knew immediately where he was. "About ten minutes. Has her water broke?" Just his luck that Taylor Tweeds, Cait's mare, took this moment to foal.

"Not yet," Cord answered just as Cait squealed in the background. "Let me take that back. Better hurry."

Dolan gassed it. Looking both ways before he proceeded, he didn't hesitate at the four way stop he encountered. Neither did he slow down until he pulled to a stop in front of Cord's stables.

Grabbing his medical bag, he wasted no time getting out of the truck and making haste. As he entered the dim building, the black mare was lying on her side. Her stomach clenched. Her wrapped tail arched as she groaned and pushed. A smooth sac protruded between the mare's vulva. Another push and the foal's front hooves appeared, one slightly ahead of the other.

"Thank God, you're here." Excitement and fear were written across Cait's taut face.

196

Cord draped his arm around her shoulder. "Honey, everything will be just fine." But even his expression looked brittle.

"Yes. But—" She swallowed hard, tears in her voice. Taylor Tweeds had lost her first colt. The mare had come into labor too early. It was only normal that Cait would be apprehensive.

Dolan forced a smile. "She'll be fine." He continued to watch the mare for any signs of distress. Finding none, he said, "She looks good."

Cait whimpered when the horse groaned in pain. "Are you going to help her?"

"It's best if these things happen naturally. Let's just watch, *quietly.*" She took Dolan's suggestion, holding tightly onto her husband.

Several minutes passed. Another contraction and the foal's legs pushed out around the knees. If there would be any problems they would usually happened around this point in the process. The nose and head should follow shortly.

Dolan waited.

The next contraction resulted without any progress. The mare's stomach heaved again—no signs of the foal's head.

He was a breath away from intervening when the mare struggled to stand, her legs shaking like rubber beneath her. The foal slid back into the mare's womb.

Cait gasped.

Surely she knew that this was normal. "Standing is the body's way of repositioning the foal, Cait," he whispered in an attempt to calm her.

Taylor Tweeds groaned, pushing to stumble back to the floor of straw.

"Cord?" Cait grabbed her husband's arm.

"Shhh, baby."

Another push and the foal's nose and head appeared. Dolan breathed a sigh of relief.

"Oh," Cait cried softly, turning in Cord's arms and hugging him.

After the head and shoulders were delivered the mare rested. Her body quivered.

"There, girl," Dolan spoke softly as he entered the clean stall lined with dry, fresh straw. He picked up a towel from a stack nearby and approached. Kneeling, he towel dried the foal's head, ensuring his nostrils and throats were clear. It was another ten minutes before the foal's rear feet appeared.

"Filly," he said.

"Yes," Cait hissed. "Are both okay?"

"Looking good."

While mother and foal rested, he got to his feet and stepped away. It was at this point that the mare transferred a large, vital amount of blood to the foal. Opening his bag he extracted his stethoscope, a large syringe filled with a mixture of Nolvasan, and a few more items he would need to examine the foal.

Cord shot Dolan a concerned look, but didn't speak until Cait walked toward the mare and filly. "Everything really okay?" he whispered.

"They're fine. Need to check the foal out more thoroughly, but they look good to me."

"How 'bout you?"

"Me?" Other than his broken heart he was fuckin' great.

"Yeah you? Tracy?" His cousin struck a chord when he said her name.

Visions of her kissing Zach popped in his head. Had she been with the sonofabitch every night he was gone? Jealousy followed pain with anger short on its heels. He just shook his head in disbelief.

"What happened?"

By the time he finished sharing all the ugly details with Cord, Taylor Tweeds had made it to her feet, breaking the umbilical cord. Her legs appeared steady as she nosed her new babe.

Dolan approached the foal that had yet to get to her feet. He eased the solution in the syringe into a small glass and set it aside as he began to examine the filly.

"Could you have misread what you saw?" Cait interrupted his thoughts as he checked the foal's eyes for pupil response.

So she had been listening.

Placing the ear tips of the stethoscope in his ears, he pressed the chest piece to the foal's damp skin and listened. "Strong heart sound and rate." Repositioning the stethoscope, he remained quiet for several seconds. "Clear lungs." When he was prepared to check the foal's mouth and leg conformation Cait spoke again.

"You know how much Zach hates you. Besides you'd have to be blind not to see Tracy is crazy about you."

"Yeah right." What did Cait know?

Retrieving the glass, he held it over the filly's umbilicus and then shook the container so that the entire stump was well coated. "I'll leave you with a handful of these syringes. You should repeat this process two or three times a day for the first forty-eight hours."

"Dolan, don't be stubborn and miss out on someone like Tracy. I mean even if she—" Cait grew quiet, quickly turning towards the foal. "So is this little baby the cutest thing you've ever seen?"

Dolan and Cord shared a knowing glance. Cait was hiding something.

"Spill it?" Dolan demanded, closing in on her.

Cait looked askew rubbing her palms on her jeans. "Are you talking to me?" Too much innocence in her voice was a dead giveaway.

"You know damn well he's talking to you." Cord had his back. "If you know something, tell him."

"It's not my place," she insisted.

Both of them nailed her with a steely glare.

She rolled her eyes. "Okay." Releasing a heavy sigh, she planted her palms on her slender hips. "Tracy has a child."

"What?" Dolan and Cord said in unison. Taylor Tweeds snorted her displeasure with their raised voices.

"Actually it's her nephew," she clarified in a whisper.

Dolan's heartbeat eased some.

"Her sister was killed in a horse accident. Tracy's the boy's guardian. For all purposes she's his mother now." Cautiously she watched Dolan.

"She never mentioned—I mean." He paused. Tracy had a child.

"Did you ever give her an opportunity?" Cait asked. "Sometimes you two are more interested in physical activities. Talking takes the backseat with you boys."

"Ah, honey." Cord reached for her.

She dodged his grasp, but Dolan saw the amusement in her eyes. "Don't, 'Ah, honey' me. It's true."

"It's just that you are so fucking sexy. I can't keep my hands off of you," Cord confessed with laughter in his tone.

Dolan could have kicked himself. Tracy had tried to talk to

him the last time they were together, but he had been more interested in physical activities as Cait put it so delicately. Had this been what Tracy had wanted to talk about or had it something to do with Zach?

"Do you love her?"

"What?" he turned his attention back to Cait.

"I said, 'Do you love her?'"

Did he? Of course he did. "The night we all had dinner together I asked her to move in with me."

Cord choked. Cait slapped her husband hard on the back.

"That's before I found her in Zach's arms." The thought made the knot in Dolan's gut twist.

"Did you let her explain?" Cait asked condescendingly. "Or did you stomp out of the room leaving her to fight off that bastard alone?"

Holy shit. Had he left her unprotected? Had Zach taken advantage of her? The fire in his blood roared to life again. He'd kill the sonofabitch.

"Soooo." Cait held on to the last letter. "You condemned her without knowing all the facts. Hung her without a trial."

Cord pulled her into his arms. "I think you got your point across, dear."

Yep. She did that quite well.

"I guess the only other question is, does it matter that she has a child?" Cait had a way of cutting through the chase and getting straight to the point.

He didn't even have to think twice. The answer was no. He wanted Tracy. If she came with a child then Dolan would welcome the boy into their lives.

"What do I do now?" The lost voice he heard didn't sound like his own, which proved he had it bad for Tracy.

201

"Grovel? Apologize? Beg?" Cait suggested with a gleam in her eyes. "Now finish checking my mare and filly and get the hell out of here."

This love thing could really hurt a man's pride. Yet when he looked at Cord gazing upon Cait with so much love, Dolan knew it was worth it.

Chapter Seventeen

Tracy needed to get out of town to reevaluate the situation. She finished washing her hands and dried them off. For two hours she had tried to get Dolan off her mind, but it did no good. The more she thought of him, the more depressed and angrier she got. He hadn't even given her a chance to explain how she wound up in Zach's arms.

As she walked out of the examination room, she recalled the fury in Dolan's eyes—eyes turned accusingly on her.

How dare he.

She swatted at the lock of hair that fell before her eyes, boots clicking against the title floor as she entered the empty waiting room. The light scent of antiseptic was present. Florence, the middle-aged receptionist, stopped typing and looked up as she passed by.

"I'll be in Dr. Zimmerman's office if you need me," Tracy threw over a shoulder.

"Yes, Dr. Marx." The click of Florence's long nails on the keyboard followed.

With each step through the sterile hallway Tracy's footsteps grew heavier. She was running away, going back to the only place she had ever felt safe—home.

Stopping before the door that sported Dr. Zimmerman's

name plate, she raised her hand and then hesitated.

Dammit. This was unprofessional and immature.

"Shake it off," she chastised as her arm lowered to her side. "Just start anew."

Which meant exactly what?

Whatever it was, she had to deal with it. This was her career. She stood a little taller. So what if she'd screwed up? She could make it right. It wasn't too late to put Dr. Crane out of her mind and focus on what was important, her career and Sheldon.

She was about to leave when the door jerked open, startling her. Zach's face was still flushed, cheeks red. He glared at her, not even attempting to camouflage his animosity.

"Move aside, boy, and let her in," Dr. Zimmerman demanded. She peered over Zach's shoulder and his father waved her in.

His son eased to the side, but not very quickly, each step a show of pain across his face. Pride squeezed her chest, knowing she had contributed to his discomfort. Her only disappointment was that she hadn't incapacitated the sonofabitch completely.

Straightening the collar of her medical jacket, she stepped inside. "I'm sorry. I thought you were alone." A variety of reasons why she might want to see him ran through her mind, but none of them seemed to work. *Think.* There had to be something they needed to discuss.

"No need for apologizes." A grey eyebrow rose. "Junior was just leaving."

"But, Dad—"

"No," he said sharply, the finality in his tone obvious. "It's a losing venture. Besides you look like you need to ice those." He glanced down at his son's crotch and then pulled his gaze toward her. "Your doings?"

Heat burned her face. Her mouth opened to respond but nothing came out. Like an idiot she just stood there.

"Fuck this," Zach growled, striking her shoulder with his as he pushed by her.

Dr. Zimmerman shook his head, a father's frustration shown in his concerned expression. "Close your mouth, dear." He limped around the big mahogany desk and took a seat.

She blinked, snapping her mouth closed. "Sir, I—"

He held up a hand. "Let me apologize for him." He inhaled and then slowly released the air in his lungs. "Are you okay?"

Lord have mercy. This must not be the first time Zach had accosted someone in the office. She was dumbfounded, searching for something intelligent to say, but the only thing that came out was, "Huh?"

Dr. Zimmerman eased back in his chair. "He's a little reckless, especially when it comes to women and Dolan. Those boys have been at each other since they were kids." Silence stretched between them. His scrutinizing stare a little unnerving. "So, did you patch things up with Dolan?"

Fuckfuckfuck. He knew about them?

She licked her lips. Her backbone straightened. "I'm not sure what you're talking about." The lie stuck in her throat.

He stared at her a moment longer. "I'm old, not blind. Not much goes on around here that I'm not privy to." He paused before adding, "Besides I was standing around the corner. Saw each of you exit the supply room. Didn't take much to put it all together."

Tracy's stomach rolled. She was going to be sick. Everything she'd worked for was slipping through her fingers. "I'm so sorry. I'll tender my resignation immediately."

He slammed a palm against the desk, making her jump. "The hell you will." He paused. His voice softened when he spoke again. "Dolan needs someone like you. The boy's lonely and misguided."

Lonely? Misguided? Were they talking about the same person?

"He's a good man." Dr. Zimmerman's expression was weary. "Solid. Just a little wild. He needs a woman who can tame him."

Tame him? She didn't want a man who needed tamed. She had responsibilities, goals. What was she thinking getting involved with him? "I'm not the one."

Dr. Zimmerman rubbed his chin. "He must think so or he wouldn't be so upset."

"His pride was bruised. He'll get over it." But could she? Could she see him every day and not yearn to touch him—kiss him?

Yes. She didn't have a choice.

He pushed his chair further beneath the desk. "We okay?"

"What about your son? I don't want any problems with him." No way did she want to fight the man every time they crossed paths. Next time he laid a hand on her she would emasculate him.

"You won't. I've asked him not to come around the office. Boy has caused enough problems." Sadness rimmed his eyes.

"Then we're good." A weight lifted from her shoulders, but she still felt exhausted from the day's events. "My schedule is clear. If you don't mind I think I'll call it a day."

Dr. Zimmerman nodded. He looked fatigued as he turned his attention to a report on his desk. Without another word she let herself out.

Standing on the other side of the closed door, she leaned against it. She could do this—she had to. Opportunity like this didn't knock every day. What happened between her and Dolan was in the past. Resolve in place, she pushed away from the door and headed for her office. As she reached for the doorknob, Courtney came around the corner, out of breath.

"Dr. Marx, Dawn's Break caught her leg in the rungs of her corral. I can't get Dr. Crane on his cell phone."

Tracy didn't think twice before releasing the door. "Let's see what she's done to herself."

Courtney led the way outside. As they turned the bend, Tracy saw Kerry holding the sorrel's halter. The filly's nostrils flared. Her eyes laden with anxiety as she danced around.

"I think she's more scared than hurt," he offered, fighting to control her. She stomped her injured leg, digging her hoof into the dirt. "Doesn't appear to be broken. But I don't know how long she had been tangled in the fence."

A light sheen of perspiration blanketed the horse's neck. The pungent scent mingled with the smell of fear. Tracy eased toward the skittish horse, jerking against the man's hold.

"Easy, girl." She hummed, growing closer. Out of the corner of her eye she saw Dolan approaching. Her attention was stolen for just a moment, but long enough that she didn't see the horse break Kerry's hold or twist and kick out with her hind leg.

It happened so quickly. Pain splintered in her head. Her feet ripped out from beneath her as darkness swallowed her up.

The breath in Dolan's lungs froze. The horse spun and kicked, her sharp hoof slamming into Tracy. Her head snapped backward, hair flying in all directions. As her feet came off the ground and she soared through the air, he hit a dead run. Landing with a sickening thud, she didn't move. Courtney released a high pitch scream. While in the background he heard Kerry struggling to get the horse under control.

Tracy's beautiful hair was matted with blood, covering her face as he fell to his knees beside her. Carefully, he brushed the hair from her eyes and the wound that bled profusely. The acrid scent was heavy in the warm air. A chill shook him.

He tried to remain calm, but his heart was pounding erratically, chest taut. It was a struggle to breathe. "Courtney, call 911." The young girl was rooted where she stood. Her eyes were panic ridden. "Courtney," he yelled.

She startled into action, running towards the facility.

Dolan's first instinct was to jerk Tracy into his arms, but he didn't dare move her in case the impact had caused a neck or spine injury. Instead he placed his hand against the wound, hoping to stop the flow that continued to leak between his fingers.

Kerry drew nearer, careful to keep the nervous horse away. "Is she okay?"

Helplessness pulled at Dolan like a drowning man forced deeper and deeper into the depths. His stomach rolled as he continued to check her vitals. His hand shook so badly, he fumbled to find a pulse. "I don't know." For a moment, he couldn't find the beat. He released her wrist and placed his fingers to her throat. Panic like he had never felt before iced his veins as he sought a palpitation. Her face was unnaturally pale. Pressing lightly on the artery just below her jaw, he felt the faint beat.

Dawn's Break whinnied and stomped her hoof. "Pen that damn horse and get me a blanket," Dolan barked. The last thing they needed was for Tracy to go into shock.

Time was elusive. Seconds seemed like minutes, minutes like hours that ripped at his heart. "Wake up, darlin'." The sound of running footsteps tore him out of the daze that had gripped him. Courtney had returned, joined by the rest of the staff, including Doc Zimmerman.

Leaning on his cane, he asked, "What happened?"

Emotion lodged in Dolan's throat as he tried to respond but couldn't. She had to be all right. If only she'd wake up. He needed to see her turquoise eyes.

"Oh." Her weak moan was the most wondrous sound he'd ever heard. Relief rushed over him like a warm breeze. She raised her arm and started to sit up, but he restrained her with his free hand.

"Be still, honey. You've been hurt."

"Hurt?" Her voice was slurred. Her eyes remained closed.

Kerry smoothed a horse blanket over her as Courtney handed him a handful of sterile bandages. He used them to apply pressure against the wound as the technician began to tell Zimmerman what had happened. By the time she finished, the cry of sirens rose. Shortly afterwards the flash of red and blue lights appeared over a hill.

As the fire truck came to abrupt stop, four firemen jumped from the vehicle. One carried a large first aid kit; another held a backboard and head immobilizer.

A tall blond man began to don latex gloves as he knelt beside Dolan. His nametag identified him as Sturgen. The fireman gave him a warm smile. "We'll take over. What happened?"

As Dolan explained the incident, Sturgen took Tracy's vitals. Another fireman removed the bandage and examined the wound. Ripping open several packages of gauze pads, he reapplied pressure against the wound while a third fireman immobilized her neck and head.

"Can you tell me your name?" Sturgen asked.

She wedged her eyes open when one of the firemen inserted an intravenous line. "Is all this necessary?"

"Darlin', answer his question." Dolan gripped her hand tightly. She frowned as if she would refuse, yet she conceded.

"Dr. Tracy Marx."

A smile tugged at the corner of his mouth. His little redhead was proud of her title. Sturgen looked toward him for confirmation.

He nodded.

"What day is it, Dr. Marx?"

"Wen—No it's Thursday."

Sturgen asked a couple more question and thankfully, she answered them clearly and correctly.

"Can you take this thing off my neck now?" she grumbled, reaching up to tug it as pain twisted her expression.

"Not until a doctor has examined you," Dolan answered before Sturgen could. She could have a concussion, internal bleeding. She wasn't coming home until he knew she was well.

"It's not n—"

"Don't argue with me. You're going to the hospital," he stated firmly. Releasing her hand, he pushed to his feet. Her precious blood was all over his hands and even his jeans and shirt. As the firemen loaded her onto the backboard and then into the back of their vehicle, he made a quick call to her uncle to let him know what happened.

As he climbed into the back of the emergency vehicle, Doc Zimmerman said, "I'll have one of the staff drive your truck to the hospital. You'll call as soon as you know something?"

"Yes." He had completely forgotten about how they'd get back home. The doors closed and he turned to find her staring at him.

"Why are you here?" she asked.

"Because it's where I belong." He leaned forward and kissed her softly.

Chapter Eighteen

The rest of the day was spent on one test after another. Night came and went. Each time a nurse woke Tracy, Dolan was there watching intently. Yet as her eyelids slid open this morning, the recliner he had been sitting in was empty. Disappointment seeped into her bones. Had it been her imagination? Had she dreamt his presence? She touched the bandage on her forehead and winced. Clearly the accident had been real as was the sterile hospital room she glanced around. The only dash of color was the beautiful flower arrangements that sat about.

Dumb. Dumb. Dumb. She couldn't believe she was in this situation. What did the doctor say? A mild concussion and eight stitches. Luck had been on her side. A chill slid up her spine, remembering the ill-fate her sister had met.

"Sheldon," she whispered, tossing back the sheet and blanket. There was so much she had to do. He was arriving on Saturday. Lord. That was tomorrow, if today was Friday. Plus she needed to check on Ice Princess and what about the office? Attempting to rise, she stopped midway when she heard the door open.

"Auntie!" Her chest tightened at the sound of her nephew's small voice, but how? She couldn't believe her eyes as the auburn-haired three-year-old bounded through the door.

Suddenly he came to an abrupt halt. Frowned and pointed to her head. "Owie."

He looked so cute. She couldn't help laughing which made her wince once more. *Owie* was right. Pain splintered to the very roots of her hair. She inhaled, pushing aside the discomfort. "How did you get here?"

Dolan stepped through the door. "I picked him up at the airport."

What? He knew about Sheldon?

"Your mother is here, too." He stepped further into the room as Sheldon ran up to the bed.

"Mom?" she choked. Tears misted her eyes. The old saying that a daughter was never too old to need her mother was true. She bit her bottom lip, trying to restrain emotion as Lois Marx entered.

Her mother was an older picture of Shelly and it made Tracy's chest constrict. Even Sheldon had their dark auburn hair and eyes like a chameleon that changed with the color of their clothes. Today her mother's eyes matched the army green shirt she wore with slacks. Sheldon's were more golden against his orange shirt.

In a scolding but relieved tone, Lois said, "Don't you ever give me a scare like that again." She moved forward and took Tracy into her arms.

Burying her face into her mother's shoulder, she inhaled the light scent of roses. "I'm sorry, Mom."

"Oh, honey." She gave her a little squeeze. "As long as you're well."

The bed moaned as Dolan set Sheldon atop it and he scrambled into their arms for a group hug. She kissed his forehead. "Have you been a good boy for Nana?"

"Yep," he chirped and then grew solemn. "Do it hurt?"

Tracy nodded.

"I sorry." Sheldon was such a sweet child. It was easy to love him and she had missed him so much, her mother too. A wave of homesickness overrode the ache in her head. Maybe it was time to go home. She fought the weepiness that swept over her.

From the corner of her eye she saw Dolan watching them. There was a heart-wrenching sadness on his face, reminding her that he had lost his family when he was very young. What was he thinking? Why had he retrieved her family when Uncle Carl could have? Why was he here?

"Thank you," she mouthed toward him as she pulled Sheldon into her lap. Her mother backed away as Dolan approached.

"How are you feeling?" Fatigue, or was it worry, showed in his eyes. His ebony hair looked like it had been finger combed this morning. He needed a shave, but he was still the most handsome man she had ever laid eyes on.

"Better. I'm ready to go home." She didn't know how a person stayed days on end in a hospital. The nurses poked and prodded her all through the night. Getting sleep was near to impossible.

"Uh. Dear," her mother said, taking a seat in the recliner. "Dolan and I were chatting."

Dolan? Her mother had certainly warmed up to him.

"I think it would be best for Sheldon and me to stay at Carl's house for a little while." She added, "You know, long enough for you to recuperate."

"Mom, it was a bump on the head. There's enough room for all of us at my house and I feel fine." Well, maybe she was fudging the truth a little. But it wouldn't take long for her to be back on her feet. Amazingly, other than the wound from the horse's hoof, she was good as new. No lingering concussion symptoms. Well, except for the nagging headache. But even that came and went. The only reasons she stayed overnight was because the doctor thought it would be wise since she'd been unconscious.

"Yes, but—"

"You need someone to take care of you," Dolan interrupted her mother.

Tracy snapped her attention toward him. "I do not. Besides I have Mom." Yes. It was true that her mother probably wouldn't be much help and it would be difficult to chase Sheldon, but they would manage.

"Honey, the flight drained me." Her mother's eyes reflected the truth. Not to mention, her face was flushed. "Sheldon can be a handful."

Brows pulled inwardly, Sheldon looked up at her. "Handful of what, Auntie?"

Tracy ruffled his hair. "A handful of mischief."

"Nah-uh," he replied, pulling away from her hand.

"Did I ever tell you how much I like mischief?" Her words drew a smile from her nephew. She turned her attention back to her mother. "So what? Did you hire me a nurse?" For a headache? How humiliating.

"Better." Her mother grinned ear to ear. "A doctor."

"Doctor? I don't understand."

"Me." Dolan pushed back her hair from her face. His touch sent chills across her skin. "You're coming home with me."

"Oh no. Uh-uh." Tracy was unwilling to drape her heart on her sleeve and leave it out there to be hurt. She had no self-control when it came to this man.

"Darlin', you don't have a choice. Your mother and I have discussed it—end of discussion."

Tracy snorted. The indelicate sound made Sheldon giggle. "The hell it is."

"Ummm. Nana, Auntie said a bad word."

"Yes she did." Dolan shook his head. "If she does it again I'll spank her," he threatened with a little growl in his voice.

Sheldon's eyelids popped open and he shrank against her. She held him closer.

"He's kidding." Tracy rubbed small circles across her nephew's back to reassure him. But the slow rise of Dolan's dark brow almost made her think differently. "Tell him you're kidding."

He leaned inward and pressed his mouth to her ear. "Don't test me." Goose bumps raised across her arms. He eased back and smiled at Sheldon. "Of course I'm teasing." He brushed the boy's head.

Damn the man. Even injured her body reacted to him. Her nipples tightened. She craved pressing her lips to his, his arms wrapped around her. That is right after she slapped the shit out of him and that smug grin.

Just then the door swung open and Uncle Carl and Laurie entered. Her cousin took one look at Dolan and melted into a puddle of teenage goo.

"Hi, Dr. Crane," she giggled, moving toward Tracy. Carl eased up beside her and she turned several shades of red. "Oh. Here." She pushed a bouquet of wildflowers into Tracy's hands. "I hope you're feeling better." She spoke not taking her eyes off of Dolan. The girl was quite smitten with the rake.

Carl frowned but turned his gaze toward Tracy. He

squeezed her hand. "Girl, what have you done to yourself?"

"It's nothing, really. Just a scratch and bump on the head."

Dolan rolled his eyes to the ceiling and she scowled at him.

"Scared the dickens out of your mother," Carl said before rubbing Sheldon's head. "Now who is this?"

The child snuggled against her. Her uncle was a stranger to him.

"Sheldon," she introduced with pride. "*My* little boy." She watched Dolan for any reaction, which didn't come. "He's come to live with me."

"Uh. Of course he has." Her uncle seemed confused. Everyone in the room already knew that but Dolan. He didn't even flinch with the revelation, pinning her with those dark eyes that made her warm inside.

"Welcome to California, little man." Carl jutted his large hand toward Sheldon. It took a moment, but the boy took it in his. After they finished shaking hands, Carl turned to his sister. "Lois."

She pushed from the recliner and rose. He met her halfway and they embraced. "It's so good to see you." Her mother's fragile body was swallowed up by Carl's much larger one.

"You too." There were tears in Lois's voice. "You said you'd keep her safe."

"Not fair," he countered. "She has a mind of her own and evidently a hard head."

"Me?" Everyone in the room laughed but Tracy.

Wrapping an arm around her shoulder, Carl hugged his sister. "Sis, I'd better get you home. C'mon little man." Dolan helped Sheldon off the bed and he ran to his Nana and grabbed her hand. "Tracy, we'll come and visit when your mother has rested." She didn't miss the concern in his eyes.

Was her mother's health worse?

Carl nailed Dolan with a heated glare. "Take care of my niece."

Dolan appeared undisturbed by Carl's aversion. "I will," he promised, taking the flowers from her hand and setting them on the table.

Her uncle wrapped his arm around her mother, guiding her and Sheldon toward the door. He pulled to a halt. "Laurie?"

"Uh, right." The teenager looked to her dad and then back at Dolan. "Maybe I should go home with Tracy and help."

"And maybe you won't." Carl jerked his head toward the door.

"Fine. Dr. Crane. Tracy, I'll come over later." Laurie sulked after them, dragging the door closed behind her.

The last thing Tracy wanted was to be left alone with Dolan. She pulled the blankets up around her like a shield. "Thank you for picking up my family." She licked her lips. "It's unnecessary for you to do anything more. I'll call Rowdy to pick me up."

"The hell you will." She startled at the firmness in his voice. "Maybe I didn't make myself clear." He drew closer making her body aware of his imposing presence. "You're coming home with me where you belong."

Belong? "No. I'm n—"

He gently pulled her into his arms, silencing her with a kiss. She wanted to fight him, but she didn't have the energy.

"I see you're doing better this morning." Dolan and Tracy jerked apart as the doctor strolled up to the bedside. Grinning, he pushed his glasses up his nose. "I'd say if you're well enough to do that then you're probably well enough to go home today. How's the head?"

Heat swarmed across her cheeks. "Head's fine." It was her lips that tingled, and her chest hurt with longing.

"Let's take a look at you," he said reaching for the stethoscope around his neck.

As the doctor examined Tracy, Dolan stood silently beside her. He should have anticipated that she would fight him. She was probably still angry from yesterday's fiasco with Zach.

Dammit. Why hadn't he reacted differently? Asked questions? Listened? Maybe killed the sonofabitch?

She wouldn't be lying in this bed right now if he'd handled things differently. Images of her crumpled on the ground, covered in blood, made him tremble with self-reproach. He could have lost her due to his pride and stubbornness.

"Now remember if you have any signs of dizziness, memory loss, nausea or vomiting, blurred vision, slurred speech, difficulty concentrating or balancing, light sensitivity, feeling anxious or irritable for no apparent reason—" she glanced at Dolan and he thought he saw her frown as the doctor continued, "—or extreme tiredness contact your family doctor immediately. Other than that I think you're good to go home."

"Alone?" she asked with a note of sarcasm.

"I don't see why not," he responded.

Dolan flashed the doctor a help-me-out-here look.

"You know it wouldn't be a bad idea to have someone around for the next couple of days," he corrected. "But you should take it easy."

Dolan got the hands-off message loud and clear. He wouldn't lie that it would be difficult, but all he wanted was to take care of her. Show her that he was sorry.

"So will you be taking care of her?" the doctor asked him.

"No," Tracy said at the same time Dolan responded, "Yes."

"I see. Remember, rest is the best thing for you."

"I'll make sure she doesn't get out of bed," Dolan promised. This time there was no doubt in his mind that she frowned at him.

As the doctor headed toward the door, Tracy turned to Dolan. "Where are my clothes?"

"Trashed."

"What?"

"They were covered in blood. I threw them away."

"Dammit. Dolan, why are you doing this? Can't you just leave me alone?" Her voice shook as if she was close to tears.

He closed the distance between them, pulling her into his arms even as she resisted. He held her at arm's length. "Darlin', I'm sorry about yesterday. I have no excuse other than jealousy. Seeing you in Zach's arms killed me."

"Of course if you had waited half a second you would have realized the bastard was accosting me—for your benefit." She batted wet eyelashes. "Oh by the way, *thanks*." Sarcasm rang in her quivering voice. "Besides, you have nothing to be jealous about. There is nothing between Zach and me or for that fact you and me." Her words were like a knife cutting straight to his heart.

The magic between them couldn't be denied. Why was she trying to push away what they had? "Do you really believe that?"

A sniffle held back the moisture in her eyes from falling. "Yes. You didn't believe me." Her response was weak, as if she might shatter at any moment. There was a moment of tight silence, and then her resolve surfaced when she shored her shoulders and raised her chin defiantly. "I have to think of

Sheldon. He's the only thing that matters, him and my career."

"We'll raise him together." The offer came so easily to him. He could raise Sheldon as his son. Emotion beat behind his eyelids. He wanted a family. Tracy. Sheldon. Lois. Somehow he would gain Carl's respect. With Cord and Cait they would be one big happy family.

"What?" Disbelief sparked in her eyes.

"I'll build a room to the house and your mother can move in too. Together we'll care for both of them."

"Do you hear what you're saying?" Before he could answer, a nurse sashayed into the room.

"You okay, Dr. Marx?" the middle-aged woman asked, carrying discharge papers in her hands and a pair of pajama bottoms and a clean robe.

"I'm fine. Thank you."

"I've called a transport." She set the change of clothing on the bed. "I thought you might need these. Your old clothes disappeared." Both women looked at him.

"She won't need those." Dolan released Tracy and went to the closet. He retrieved one of the boxes he had hidden in there earlier. "This is for you." He handed the white box with a lacy ribbon around it to Tracy.

She didn't open it, just stared at him with an expression of disbelief, until the nurse said, "Wonderful, something brand new to go home in. After we go through the doctor's instructions you're free to leave."

It took only minutes for the nurse to relay the doctor's orders, and then she was gone, leaving them alone. With a brush of Tracy's hand she pushed aside the red bow and opened the box. A white satin and chiffon slip and matching cover-up slid through her fingers. "You shouldn't have." As she shoved the tissue paper aside, a pair of slippers fell out of the box. "There's no panties."

"Whoops." He feigned innocence. The matching underwear was safely in one of his jean pockets. "Guess you'll have to go without." His cock twitched with the thought of her bare skin beneath the flimsy material.

"Or I could wear these pajama bottoms." She held up the boring hospital garment.

He hadn't expected that complication. Reaching into his pocket, he pulled out the satiny briefs and waved them like a white flag of surrender, which won him the first smile since this horrible incident happened. As he handed them to her, he said, "I'm sorry about Zach. Let me prove it to you. Come home with me and I'll take care of you."

She closed her eyes briefly. "Dolan—"

"Please, Tracy." He heard desperation in his own voice. "Give me—us a chance. A couple of days are all I'm asking for." He reached for her. "I love you."

Her expression dropped as the color in her face drained. He wasn't sure if that was a good thing or not.

She licked her lips. Nervous.

Good or bad sign?

He waited for her to say something—anything.

"I really need some clothes." Not quite what he expected, but he had that covered too.

Walking back to the closet, he picked up a paper sack. "I hope you don't mind. I retrieved your purse from the office and found your house key. There's a couple of things in there for you to choose from."

"Thank you." Rummaging through the sack, she chose the sundress and matching sandals he had selected. Without asking for his assistance, she quickly donned the outfit. Silence lingered between them until the transporter came with the wheelchair.

As he followed behind them, pushing a cart laden with her flowers, he realized Cait was right. It looked like there would be a helluva lot of apologizing, groveling and begging on his part before Tracy forgave him.

Chapter Nineteen

A steady stream of well-wishers arrived shortly after Dolan settled Tracy on the couch in his house. He fluffed a pillow, placing it behind her back, and followed it up with an afghan tucked snuggly around her. It was a sweet gesture, but she was still speechless from his previous avowal.

He loved her. She couldn't quite get her arms around it.

If that hadn't thrown her into a tizzy, then the fact that she was staying at his home, which let the cat out of bag about them, did. She didn't miss the curious expressions exchanged between Courtney and Beth or the pleasant smirk on Dr. Zimmerman's mouth as he swayed back and forth in the rocking chair near the fireplace.

"Quite a goose egg you got there, dearie," he said. "Nearly half a horseshoe by my reckon." He was exaggerating, of course, since the tip of the horse's hoof connected with her forehead. He was correct about the swelling. Add the black and blue coloring and the knitted stitches across her forehead and she looked like she was preparing for Halloween.

"Damn horse," Dolan muttered more to himself than anyone else. "Are you warm enough?" He checked the blanket for the nth time, cocooning her. She pulled her arms from beneath to break the stifling feeling that began to surround her. Her mind was whirling, pulse racing with his nearness. There was so much they needed to discuss, but it would have to wait until they were alone. For now she focused on not allowing anyone else to know that there was more on her mind than a bump on the head.

"How is Dawn's Break?" she asked, wishing Dolan would quit fussing over her. It bordered on embarrassment as he stood sentry next to her. Yet there was no denying his attentiveness touched her heart. The roguish rake had a domestic bone. Every woman's dream come true, including hers.

Courtney walked toward the window seat and sat. "Her ankle swelled a little. She has some scrapes and bruises, but Dr. Zimmerman thinks she'll do just fine. Everyone was more concerned about you. You gave us quite a scare."

"I'm so sorry. I looked away for only a second." Dolan placed a warm palm on her shoulder and squeezed. She glanced up at him and saw guilt swimming in his eyes. It wasn't his fault, it was hers. Hell. This whole mess was due to her need for adventure. But what an adventure it had been. The peaceful sensation that swept over her vanished when the unthinkable invaded her mind.

Was he doing all of this because he felt responsible for her accident? Men had no problem using the "L" word when it suited their purpose. The thought made her stomach roll and none too quietly.

"Hungry?" he whispered.

"No. Thank you."

"You haven't eaten today," he insisted.

"Neither have you." She grew quiet when she realized all eyes were on them. Beth had joined Courtney on the window seat. They smiled knowingly at her. Evidently this domestic side of Dr. Crane they had never seen.

He must have felt their stare because he changed the subject. "Can I get anyone something to drink?"

Courtney and Beth shook their heads. Their inquisitive gazes pinned on his every move as he fondled Tracy's hair between his fingers. Beth giggled and whispered something Tracy couldn't hear.

Great. Rumors would be flying by this evening.

Dr. Zimmerman tapped his cane on the floor. "I'll take a scotch. It's after twelve," he rationalized. "I consume a little from time to time for medicinal purposes."

Yeah right.

Tracy couldn't help smiling. "I'll take one of those too." She could use a stiff drink or two.

"When did the doctor say you could come back to work?" he asked.

Muscles rippled beneath Dolan's T-shirt as he walked toward the kitchen. Damn the man was good-looking. "Maybe a week. I'll know more after I see a doctor next week. Anyone you would suggest?"

Dr. Zimmerman was providing a rundown of the doctors in Santa Ysabel when Dolan returned. He handed Dr. Zimmerman his drink before he went to her side and handed her a glass. She took a sip and puckered at the tart flavor.

Lemonade?

She looked askew at him. "Yuck!"

"No alcohol per your doctor's instructions," he chided, returning to his place beside her.

Wonderful. Now he was her guardian? Men could be so pushy, especially this hardheaded one.

Rapping on the front door pulled his attention from her and to whoever stood on the other side. He excused himself. Quickly she disposed of her glass on the end table. She hated lemonade.

Female laughter caught her attention as Caitlyn and Cord stepped into the room holding a beautiful leafy plant. As Cord approached, saw her head, he flinched. "Ouch." Setting the fern next to the fireplace, he drew nearer. "That looks like it hurts."

"Thank God you're okay." Caitlyn pushed the baking pan she held into Dolan's empty hands. "I brought you a chicken casserole. It just needs to be heated, three-fifty. You can do that, can't you, Dolan?" She winked at Tracy and then leaned close to give her a gentle hug.

Chicken. Who would have guessed? Tracy silently chuckled. She liked Caitlyn, even if she had a poultry fetish. "Thank you."

Dolan caught her eye and his smile sent warmth through her veins. She couldn't help wondering how this would play out. He was everything she'd dreamt of. A man who cared and made her body burn, but more importantly he was willing to raise Sheldon. He had even offered to welcome her mother into his home. But was it for real?

The couch dipped as Caitlyn sat, empathy in her expression. "How are you doing?"

Tracy pulled her feet beneath her, making more room. "As long as I don't touch my head, I'm fine." Her pain appeared centralized around the injury. Plus she had no headaches or blurred vision. Of course, her entire body ached, but that was probably due to the impact of the fall. In fact, at the hospital when she changed into her clothes, she had noticed a large bruise on her hip. It hadn't looked any better when she donned the white satin and chiffon slip and cover-up Dolan had insisted she change into when they arrived.

"I hear your nephew and mother arrived. Dolan picked them up at the airport." She waited a heartbeat before saying,

"So?" Tracy could tell by the smile on her new friend's face, she was bursting at the seams for information.

Thump. Thump. Saved by the bell, or should she say knock. Someone else announced their arrival by pounding on the door. Dolan opened it and Sheldon shot by him, his little feet moving like lightning as he ran around the couch and straight into Tracy's arms.

Laurie was close behind him, but she pulled to halt in front of Dolan.

"Hi, Dr. Crane."

Tracy rolled her eyes. Here they go again.

She hugged her nephew close. "This is my boy." Pride filled her chest as she pulled him into her lap. "Sheldon, I want you to meet Mrs. Daily."

"Cait," she said warmly. "What a gorgeous young man."

"Thank you," he said, giving Tracy another reason why she thought he was the most wonderful child in the world.

The noise level in the room elevated as her uncle Carl, carrying a large sack, entered. "I hope you're all hungry." The scent of fried chicken filled the room. "Laurie, get your butt into the kitchen and help me." He was followed by her mother, who had a big chocolate cake in her hands.

Laurie frowned at her father's words, shoulders dropping as she sulked all the way into the kitchen.

It looked like a party was about to break out.

Before the door closed, Rowdy waltzed in. He shook hands with Dolan, and then he headed straight for her. "You okay, baby?" Neither his endearment nor his caring expression escaped their watchful audience.

A hush fell over the room.

An awkward moment ensued until Sheldon jumped off her

lap. "Nana, can I have cake?" Chocolate was his favorite. Without waiting for a response he took off for the kitchen.

Rowdy turned to Caitlyn. "I hear you and Cord finally got hitched." As Cord joined them, they drifted away from the couch.

"I'd better go help," Dolan said.

"We'll help, too," Courtney offered. Both women stood and followed him into the other room while Dr. Zimmerman continued to rock, sipping from his glass with a look of amusement on his weathered face as he looked from Rowdy to her.

His previous words came back to her. *Not much goes on around here that I'm not privy to.*

She couldn't help wondering if his knowledge expanded beyond the office. Did he know about the threesome arrangement she had with Dolan and Rowdy? Dolan's reputation appeared to be well known. Lost in thought, she didn't hear her mother's approach.

She sat at Tracy's feet. "How are you feeling?"

Tracy was getting a little tired, her eyelids growing heavy. "I'm good."

Her mother looked around the room. "Is the crowd bothering you? Would you rather sleep?"

In Dolan's bed? Probably not a good idea.

"There's plenty of time to sleep." She reached out and took her mother's hand. "It's wonderful having you here."

Lois glanced at Dr. Zimmerman. In a hushed tone, she asked, "Are you good with this arrangement?"

"Truthfully?" Tracy paused. Her heart leaped when Dolan entered the room holding Sheldon in his arms. "I don't know." Instead of cake, the boy held a plate overflowing with food, too much food for such a little guy.

Dolan set Sheldon on his feet and her nephew went to her side. Displeasure twisted his small features.

"What's wrong?" she asked.

"Have to eat 'fore cake."

She reached out and stroked his arm. "Who says?"

He jutted a finger toward Dolan. "Him."

She stifled the chuckle that tickled her throat. "You know, honey, he's right. But that's a lot of food for a little boy." Dolan couldn't possibly think Sheldon could eat all of that.

Her nephew pushed the plate toward her. "It's for you."

"Me?" She swung her feet toward the floor and sat up before she took the plate.

Sheldon frowned at Dolan. "*He* says you gotta eat." It appeared the two of them had gotten off on the wrong foot. Evidently, chocolate cake stood between them.

Her mother rose from the couch. "Come on, grandson. Let's go fix you a plate."

Dr. Zimmerman pushed from the rocker. "I think I'll join them."

Alone, Dolan sat next to Tracy. "You look tired." He brushed a fallen tendril from her forehead and away from her wound near her hairline. The tremor that shook her didn't go unnoticed. Did his touch affect her as much as hers did him?

"I'm fine." The dark circles beneath her eyes revealed differently. Even still she was the most beautiful woman he had ever laid eyes on.

His palms itched with the need to reach out to her. "You need to eat." It was killing him not to touch her, take her into his arms and hold her as she drifted off to sleep.

She looked down at the laden plate. "I can't possibly eat all this."

"Try," he coaxed.

She cocked a brow. "Or what? I don't get any cake?"

Was she upset with him? He pushed his fingers through his hair. "I'm sorry. I just thought he should—I don't think your nephew likes me."

Laughter danced in her eyes. "Cake is pretty important to a three-year-old."

Relief brushed over him. He would have to be blind not to recognize she adored the boy. Sheldon could very well be the key to her heart. Dolan wanted that key safely in his possession. "Eat."

She picked up a fried chicken leg and handed it to him. "Only if you help me."

A smile tugged at his mouth as he accepted her offering. He waited until she took a bite before he did. A mixture of spices and the succulent juice of the chicken burst upon his tongue. He had never tasted anything so delicious. "Damn. That's good."

She finished chewing and then swallowed. "It's Mom's special recipe."

Not thinking, he said, "We'll have to get the recipe." He didn't miss her expression as it grew serious. The distance between them thickened.

Setting the plate on the end table, she turned around and a sober expression fell across her face. "I have to consider Sheldon. What's right for him. He needs a stable environment, a mother and father who he can count on."

He placed the chicken leg on the plate. "What exactly do you think I'm suggesting?"

"Well." She floundered for only a moment. "For me—us to

move in with you, here." Wariness shadowed her eyes, uncertainty lurking in their depths. "What will people say? How will their comments affect Sheldon? Our careers?"

He wanted—expected so much more, especially from her. He wanted her heart and soul. "I don't want you to just occupy the rooms in this house." His voice rose with frustration.

Uncertainty darkened her eyes. "Then what do you want?" Her voice trembled as color dotted her cheeks with what looked like embarrassment.

This conversation was not going in the direction he had anticipated. "You. A home."

Silence stretched between them.

"Dammit, Tracy." Nervously, he flexed his fingers then curled them into fists to keep from reaching for her and giving her a firm shake. "If I have to get on my fuckin' knees, I will. I want you to marry me."

Several gasps from across the room made him freeze. This couldn't be happening. Slowly he turned around.

Holy shit.

Half their visitors stood just inside the living room holding plates of food and expressions of surprise.

Carl looked as if someone had just jabbed him with a cattle prod, while his daughter's expression was as if the world had come to an end. Courtney held her hand over her mouth. Cait's eyes beamed with excitement, while Lois's grew moist.

Cord shook his head. "Damnedest proposal I've ever heard."

Cait elbowed him in the side. "Shhh…"

"Proposal?" Dr. Zimmerman asked strolling into the room, carrying a plate in one hand, his cane in the other.

"Dr. Crane just proposed to Dr. Marx," Courtney whispered.

"Atta'boy."

"What's going on?" Beth asked, stepping into the room.

Dr. Zimmerman headed for the rocking chair. "We're having a celebration. Dolan and Tracy are getting married."

"Married?" Rowdy repeated, entering with Sheldon beside him.

Dolan braved a glance toward Tracy. Slack jawed, she looked stunned, flinching when all the women descended upon her. How it happened he wasn't sure, but they maneuvered him off the couch, surrounding her. Everyone chatted at once.

A slap on the back jerked him out of his stupor. "Congratulations." Rowdy extended his hand. He saw no animosity on his friend's face as they shook hands.

His felicitations were followed by Cord's and the rest of the men, except for Carl who frowned. "You better do my niece right, Crane."

"I will," Dolan responded, wondering if he'd get the chance. Tracy still hadn't agreed to marry him, even if everyone else had assumed her answer was yes.

He felt a tug on his pant leg and looked down. Big innocent eyes looked up at him. Something took hold of his heart and squeezed. This little guy would be his son.

Sheldon held an empty plate in his hand. "Can I have cake now?"

He retrieved the empty plate and set it upon an end table before he bent down and hauled the boy into his arms. "You sure can. How big a piece do you want?"

"Big," he yelled, throwing up his hands and catching Tracy's attention. She looked worried. The tension in her face eased slightly when Sheldon wrapped his little arms around Dolan's neck. There were a series of female, *ahhh's*, but the only one he cared about was Tracy's.

"Okay, buddy. Let's go."

In the kitchen he sat Sheldon on a chair and headed for a drawer to get a knife.

"Do you have a horse?" the child asked, watching him as he began to slice the cake. "Bigger."

"Are you sure you can eat a larger piece?"

He nodded. "Do you have a horse?"

Dolan slid the knife beneath the slice of cake and placed it on a plate along with a fork. "I do." He set the dessert before the boy and he immediately picked up his fork and began to eat.

With his mouth full, he mumbled. "Auntie won't let me ride."

That was understandable, but this was a ranch. Tracy would need to get past her fears.

"Need some help?" Lois stood in the doorway. A soft expression fell across her face when she looked at her grandson.

"I think I've got it under control." But he wasn't sure. He'd never been around children. This would be a new experience for him. Again, he tried to remind himself that Tracy had yet to agree to marry him.

"Do you love her?" He should have expected that question from Lois.

Not hesitating, he said, "Yes."

A troubled look furrowed her forehead. "She's been through so much and she has a lot of responsibility." Her gaze went to Sheldon. "She can't afford to make a mistake."

"I understand," he said. "Your daughter hasn't agreed to marry me."

"I know." A smile brightened her eyes. "She will."

"How can you be so sure?" He held onto the woman's words with hope.

"She wouldn't be here if she didn't care about you." She glanced again at Sheldon. The boy was covered in chocolate and still pushing the dessert into his mouth.

"You know that you're welcome to live with us."

"Thank you." Lois dragged in a heavy breath. "Carl has asked me to stay as well. I think I might just take him up on his invitation. Maybe keep an eye on you." She winked. "Now why don't you let me take care of this little heathen. It sounds like you have some work to do."

That was putting it lightly. As he wiped his hands on a towel, he figured tonight would be extremely interesting.

Chapter Twenty

Nothing lay between Dolan and Tracy but the night and words left unspoken. A dim light from the master bathroom bled into the room, casting shadows around his bedroom. She hugged up to her pillow, smelling his spicy cologne upon it.

How had things gotten so out of control?

In everyone's eyes she was as good as bound to the man who lay silently against her back. The warmth of his naked body radiated straight through the thin material of her slip, making it hard for her think. She closed her eyes and her mother's smiling face appeared. She had embraced the idea of her daughter's marriage, giving her blessings, while Caitlyn had even begun to make plans for the upcoming nuptials. Together, they had even settled on a date. It had been a chaotic moment, one that left Tracy's head buzzing.

She opened her eyes, staring across the room. She was glad when everyone had departed, except that left her and Dolan alone. Strangely, they had moved through the steps of getting ready for the evening and then climbed into bed without a word.

How ironic. They were already acting like a married couple with something wedged between them. Yet the question of marriage was the "something".

Excitement and fear made strange bedfellows.

He was everything she had ever wanted. Still she couldn't

help but wonder if their love was a passing phase. Hell. They hadn't even known each other for what? Two weeks. What happened when their lust cooled? Would they still have something substantial to hold on to? Did they have enough between them to build forever upon? She couldn't make another mistake—not this time.

"Penny for your thoughts." His smooth voice slid over her skin as his hand glided up her arm making goose bumps flare.

She licked her lips. "What are we going to do?"

He scooted back and rolled her upon her back. Cradling her face in his palms, he looked deep in her eyes. "Marry me."

A dark lock of hair fell upon his forehead. She couldn't help raising her hand and brushing it away. "We don't know each other."

"I know I've never felt this way about anyone. I crave every inch of you against my skin."

"That's lust, not love."

"Tracy, please." He paused briefly. "I'm not good at expressing my feelings." She heard him swallow hard. "Dammit, woman," he breathed. "You mess with my head. You're in my dreams, my thoughts. I can't bear it when we're separated. Just the thought of another man touching you is like a knife in my gut." There was so much emotion in his words, tears moistened her eyes. Gently he stroked her cheek with the back of his hand. "Can't you see that I love you?"

She needed to believe him.

While she struggled with the knowledge that the odds were against them, that love at first sight was as impossible as improbable, she wanted to take what he offered because she loved him too. Yet instead of expressing her love, letting him know that the feeling was mutual, she said, "Prove it."

"What?" There was almost a lost boy quality to his voice. "How? What can I do?"

Wrapping her arms around his neck, she pulled him close, their lips almost touching. "Make love to me." Her body ached to feel him deep inside her.

"We can't—shouldn't." Even as he spoke, she felt his cock harden and press against her leg. Her nipples beaded in response.

"I need you," she admitted without shame. More than anything, she had to know the love they felt was real. Something that felt so perfect had to be right.

He pulled into a sitting position, forcing her to release her hold on his head. She felt his hands shake as he fisted them into her slip and began to raise the hem. Pushing the gown up her body, he revealed the thong she wore. His gaze was pinned on her as he continued to expose her breasts, up further until she was completely disposed of the garment. With a flick of his wrist he sent the satin floating on the air.

"Baby." His breathy endearment discharged a firebolt between her thighs that traveled to her belly. He inched the thong down her hips and rays of sensation burst from her nipples to make her breasts throb, growing heavy.

"Dolan." His name was a whisper on her lips as she reached for him.

He fell into her arms, wedging his knee between her legs as he eased his weight upon her. She felt the tremor that filtered through him. He captured her mouth. Feather-light, he kissed her with such tenderness that it humbled her to know how much he desired her.

"Mine," he murmured against her lips.

"Forever," she returned, eliciting a surprising growl from him, before he went perfectly still.

"Fuck," he groaned.

What now? She was afraid to ask. His firm erection twitched against her damp folds. She couldn't bear the thought of something coming between them—not now.

"I—I want you so badly." Another tremor assailed him. He tensed, every muscle clenching beneath her touch. "Don't know if I can be gentle or hold on for long."

Relief and love washed over her in waves. "Then let me take the reins, cowboy. Where's your slicker?"

"Slicker?"

"Condom." She placed her palms on his chest, smooth skin and iron hardness, and then she pushed, rolling him off her and onto his back.

"In the top drawer of the bedstand."

Inching off the bed, she wasted no time retrieving the package. With her teeth she tore open the package, extracted the sheath and finally placed the paper inside the wastebasket. Crawling back upon the bed, she slinked toward him. As she circled her fingers around his cock, he growled. The deep raspy sound was so sexy she tightened her grip and stroked.

"Darlin'—"

"*Shhh...*" Carefully she slid the latex over his cock and then straddled him. Leaning forward to angle her hips, she positioned the tip of his cock to the opening of her body. With one thrust she impaled herself upon him.

"Oh God," she cried out as he raised his hips and filled her completely.

Tiny sparks of heat thrummed through Dolan's body as her pussy slid over him like a glove. Warm. Wet. Tight. He prayed for strength to hold on as he grasped her narrow hips.

The slow, steady pace she began was so fuckin' amazing it was all he could do not to explode. A shiver slid up his spine. He reached for her breasts needing something to focus on instead of the heat pounding in his groin.

As he pinched her nipples between his fingers, her mouth parted on a soft whimper. Yet it wasn't his touch that made her eyelids grow heavy. This position allowed for deeper penetration while her clit rubbed against his body, stimulating the organ.

Good for her—hell for him.

Each stroke teased the sensitive head of his cock, sending blood roaring toward his crotch. A thread of fire lanced down his erection. His breath hitched. "Easy, darlin'." He was lucky just to get those words out. His voice was taut and coarse. His body a rocket ready to erupt.

His little redheaded vixen had other things in mind as she continued to ride him, holding his restraint in the palm of her hand.

"Feels. So. Good." She angled her hips and pressed down hard against him.

Dolan's entire body twitched and then tensed. "Fuck," he groaned, fighting the burn that made his toes feel like they actually curled. The edge of pain and pleasure caught him in its grasp. He couldn't hold on for much longer.

"Yes," she hissed, picking up the rhythm. "God yes." Her back arched. Her breathing came in short, quick pants to match his. The end was rushing in for both of them.

The second her inner muscles clamped down, milking him, it was all over. Lightning ripped down his cock, tearing a cry from his diaphragm. He grasped her hips, trying to control her, ease her bucking motion, but she was caught in the grips of her climax. Cherishing each of her small cries, he held on to her and together they rode the wave, their bodies locked in what could only be described as ecstasy.

As she collapsed upon him, he wrapped his arms around her and held on like he would never let her go. In the quiet that surrounded them, he could feel her heart beating, throbbing to the rhythm of his own.

A sense of calmness embodied him. The loneliness, emptiness he had experienced most of his life seemed to dissipate into thin air. He couldn't wait to fall asleep like this each night and wake each morning in her arms. Soon he would have a family—a real one consisting of a wife, a son, a mother-in-law, and in time perhaps a daughter with flaming red hair like her mother's. The thought brought tears to the surface. Moisture rolled down his cheek and he silently prayed she didn't see it.

Grappling with his emotion, he cleared his throat. "So when should we do this?" *The sooner the better,* he left that part unspoken.

Laughter burst from her lips as she raised her head. "Now that was really romantic."

Remorse slapped him in the face. "Shit. I'm sorry. It's just—"

She snuggled against him. "Maybe we should take it easy. Consider a lengthy engagement."

Disappointment hit him hard. He thought about it for the thump of a heartbeat. "Not gonna work."

She eased up out of his embrace. Rolling to her side, she asked, "Why?"

He leaned upon his side so that they faced each other. "Because I get the feeling you don't plan to move in with me until after we're married."

"It would be best for Sheldon."

"Then waiting won't work," he said flatly. "Don't ask me to wait." Dammit. He couldn't.

She rested her head on a palm. "What's your suggestion?"

Cord and Caitlyn had run off to Las Vegas and got hitched the next day. If it was up to Dolan they'd do the same. Yet he had seen the excitement in Tracy's mother's face and the dreamy expression Cait had when she talked about the wedding dress and ring.

Shit. He hadn't even purchased her a ring. "I'm told it's all about the wedding dress and ring. Guess we could wait until you found the right dress."

She speared her fingers through his hair and drew him close. "You heard wrong." Her lips were soft against his as she whispered, "It's all about the man. Fuck the wedding dress and ring. Been there—done that. How about Las Vegas?"

A mile-wide grin fell across his face. "Really?"

"Really. I don't need anything but you." She eased upon her back. "Now, cowboy." She stretched like a cat. With that sexy voice that always slid across his skin like silk, she said, "Take me again."

As Dolan crawled atop Tracy, he knew he had found the woman of his heart. No more lonely nights or unfilled dreams. Together they would be a family and make a house a home.

"Thank you," he whispered.

About the Author

A taste of the erotic, a measure of daring and a hint of laughter describe Mackenzie McKade's novels. She sizzles the pages with scorching sex, fantasy and deep emotion that will touch you and keep you immersed until the end. Whether her stories are contemporaries, futuristics or fantasies, this Arizona native thrives on giving you the ultimate erotic adventure.

When not traveling through her vivid imagination, she's spending time with three beautiful daughters, three devilishly handsome grandsons, and the man of her dreams. She loves to write, enjoys reading, and can't wait 'til summer. Boating and jet skiing are top on her list of activities. Add to that laughter and if mischief is in order—Mackenzie's your gal!

To learn more about Mackenzie, please visit www.mackenziemckade.com. Send an email to Mackenzie at mackenzie@mackenziemckade.com or sign onto her Yahoo! group to join in the fun with other readers and authors as well as Mackenzie!

http://groups.yahoo.com/group/wicked_writers/

There's nothing casual about this caper...

Private Property
© *2009 Leah Braemel*

Jodi Tyler has loved and lost too many times to believe in happily ever after. That's what makes her no-strings affair with her boss so perfect—his power in bed matches his respect for her independence. Still, when he surprises her with a ménage for her birthday, her secret thrill wars with a nagging thought: Why would he so casually share her with another man?

Even though Mark Rodriguez holds Jodi at arm's length from his heart, her self-confidence is a turn-on he can't resist. Inviting old college buddy and future business partner Sam into their bed for one night was supposed to set free her wildest fantasy. Instead he finds the tables turned, forced to watch while Sam brings her to the height of ecstasy.

Now, Mark's not so sure he wants to share his treasure...

Warning: This book contains a woman fulfilling her sexual fantasies—including two men who are happy to tie her up, and be tied up, while using graphic language and floggers.

Available now in ebook from Samhain Publishing.

*She'll do whatever it takes to get to the top
of the professor's learning curve.*

Tamed
© *2008 Lynne Maris*

Katrina Keens has discovered the man she longs for,
Professor Derek Jacobson, is a Dom. Though BDSM is
something she's never tried, the idea of submitting to Derek is
darkly arousing. All she needs is one chance to slip past the
strict student-professor boundary he has been unwilling to
breach.

And now that opportunity has come, a way to show Derek
that she can be the woman he needs. Without waiting for his
permission.

Unaware of her identity at a masked sex party, he offers
Katrina everything she's dreamed of—to be her master for the
night, teasing her with a promise of intensely arousing
discipline and praise.

Only Derek is a demanding master. Learning to serve his
needs is a ruthless lesson in pleasure she won't soon forget.

*Warning: Contains graphic language, bondage, toys, anal
play, and sexual encounters in public settings.*

Available now in ebook from Samhain Publishing.

Ridin' the edge of lust is fun—until someone falls in love.

Cowgirl Up and Ride
© *2008 Lorelei James*
A Rough Riders book.

Goody-two boots AJ Foster has waited her entire life for her dream cowboy Cord McKay to see her as more than the neighbor girl in pigtails. Now that she's old enough to stake her claim on him, she's pulling out all the sexual stops and riding hell-bent for leather—straight for his libido.

Divorced rancher Cord has sworn off all women...until innocent AJ suggests he teach her how to ride bareback—and he realizes she doesn't mean horses or bulls. Between his responsibilities running his massive ranch, missing his young son and dealing with the sexual shenanigans of his brother and cousins, Cord is more than willing to take AJ up on her offer. On a trial basis.

The fun and games tie them both up in knots. AJ isn't willing to settle for less than the whole shootin' match with her western knight. But for Cord, even though the sexy cowgirl sets his blood ablaze, he's determined to resist her efforts to lasso his battered heart.

Sweet, determined AJ has the power to heal—or heel—the gruff cowboy...unless Cord's pride keeps him from admitting their relationship is more than a simple roll in the hay.

Warning: this book contains: raunchy sex scenes that'll work you into a lather faster than a winded horse, graphic language, resourceful use of baling twine, ménage a trois, ménage a quatage, and yippee! hot nekkid man-on-man-lovin'.

Available now in ebook and print from Samhain Publishing.

GREAT CHEAP FUN

Discover eBooks!

THE FASTEST WAY TO GET THE HOTTEST NAMES

Get your favorite authors on your favorite reader, long before they're out in print! Ebooks from Samhain go wherever you go, and work with whatever you carry—Palm, PDF, Mobi, and more.

Samhain
publishing
Ltd

WWW.SAMHAINPUBLISHING.COM

Lightning Source UK Ltd.
Milton Keynes UK
02 March 2011

168511UK00001B/143/P